The Huggabie Falls trilogy

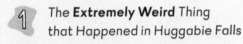
Adam Cece lives in Adelaide with his family. He has always liked wondering about weird things, so he decided to write a book about a place where the very weirdest things happen. Then he decided to write a sequel.

adamcece.com

Andrew Weldon is a cartoonist based in Melbourne. He has written and illustrated several books for children.

andrewweldon.com

Adam Cece

the
UNBELIEVABLY
SCARY
THING THAT
HAPPENED IN
HUGGABIE
FALLS

illustrated by
Andrew Weldon

TEXT PUBLISHING MELBOURNE AUSTRALIA

WITHDRAWN

textpublishing.com.au
textpublishing.co.uk

The Text Publishing Company
Swann House, 22 William Street, Melbourne, Victoria 3000, Australia

The Text Publishing Company (UK) Ltd
130 Wood Street, London EC2V 6DL, United Kingdom

First published by The Text Publishing Company, 2018.

Book design by Imogen Stubbs.
Illustrations © Andrew Weldon.
Typeset by Text.

Printed and bound in Australia by Griffin Press, an Accredited ISO AS/NZS 14001:2004 Environmental Management System printer.

ISBN: 9781925773019 (paperback)
ISBN: 9781925626964 (ebook)

A catalogue record for this book is available from the National Library of Australia.

For Albert and Edward.
Courage.
Love.
Uncles.
The three most important things in life.

1

The Trouble with Sequels

If you've picked up this book—which I assume you have, otherwise how are you even reading this—then I'm sorry to tell you that this is a sequel. It's the sequel to *The Extremely Weird Thing that Happened in Huggabie Falls*, which of course was a spectacular book, written by the equally spectacular, devilishly handsome and stupendously modest author, named me. But while that book was a masterpiece, who knows whether this one will be as good?

In fact, I was against writing a sequel. But so many kids have written to me wanting to know what happened next in Huggabie Falls that I found myself crumbling under the pressure.

So I have dusted off my typewriter, and cleared off the mess on my desk, and I've started writing about another thing that happened in Huggabie Falls, which is quite a coincidence, because something unbelievable just happened in Huggabie Falls, something so unbelievable I scarcely believe it myself.

But the fact that I can scarcely believe what happened isn't the biggest problem I have. The biggest problem with writing a sequel is that some of the people who pick up the sequel have not read the first book. If you are one of those people, then I'd like to ask you what the blazes you think you're playing at? I think you should take a good long hard look at your reading habits.

So for those people—you know who you are—I'll summarise the first book: the extremely

2

weird thing that happened in the extremely weird town of Huggabie Falls was by far the weirdest thing that had ever happened anywhere. It was the spread of normality, and Kipp Kindle and his two best friends, Tobias Treachery and Cymphany Chan, realised that they didn't want their town to become normal, even though they once did, because being weird turned out to be the best thing about their town. So they had to fight the evil thin man Felonious Dark and an evil creepy scientist, whose name I can't remember, and her henchmen, who weren't so much evil as just paid to do a job. And I don't want to ruin anything here, but Kipp, Tobias and Cymphany won, and *urgghhh*...my brain has already turned to jelly so if you want to know any more then you'll just have to go and read the first book. I mean, I've said it before and I'll say it again, what are you playing at?

Addendum: my publisher has asked that I refrain from insulting and badgering readers about their reading-order habits and that I should express the opinion that readers can read books in any order they like, which sounds just crazy but I'm willing to be proven wrong, even though I've never been proven wrong before.

Now, where was I? Oh yes—the next thing that happened in Huggabie Falls. Kipp, Tobias and Cymphany, fresh from putting a stop to the extremely weird thing that happened in Huggabie Falls, were back in their normal lives. Or as normal as your life can be when you have a teacher who is a witch and, in Kipp's case, everyone in your family is cursed to turn invisible at puberty, and, in Tobias's case, your family is so deceitful and distrustful that you have to board up the doors and windows of your house to keep out angry debt collectors. Cymphany's life, on the other hand, was almost actually back to normal, because her family was the most normal family in all of Huggabie Falls anyway, as the only weirdness in her family was that her father stood on a little bit of a lean.

Kipp, Tobias and Cymphany were having lunch at the Huggabie Falls Sanctuary for People Fleeing from Witches and Other Dangerous Flying Creatures, on Digmont Drive. They weren't there trying to flee from their teacher, Ms Turgan, flying on her broom, although ordinarily that would have been a good reason to go there—they were there because the sanctuary's cafe had some of the best doughnuts in town.

Kipp was looking at his hand and frowning. 'You don't think I'm starting to turn invisible, do you?' He held his hand up. 'Look at the back of my hand. Does that look glistening and translucent to you?'

Tobias looked carefully at his worried friend's hand. 'It's clear icing,' he said, 'from the doughnut.'

Kipp licked his hand, and the relief on his face was instantaneous.

Cymphany laughed. 'I'm so glad everything

is back to normal—or back to weird. I'd be happy if nothing else ever happened in Huggabie Falls.'

Tobias nodded. 'I wouldn't worry. After the extremely weird thing that happened, I don't think anything else could happen.'

At that exact moment a blood-curdling scream ripped through the Huggabie Falls Sanctuary for People Fleeing from Witches and Other Dangerous Flying Creatures. It was so loud, and so forceful, that it pushed Kipp, Tobias and Cymphany's hair up, making little upright walls on the tops of their heads.

Kipp glared at his friends, as if to say, why did you say that, why did you tempt fate?

'To tempt fate' is an expression that means the more you say something will never happen, the more likely it is that the thing will happen. I tempted fate once, when I said, 'I bet I'll never, ever, in a million billion years, write a sequel to *The Extremely Weird Thing that Happened in Huggabie Falls.*' And so, case in point, I think you get what I mean.

Froggin Fillibuster, the proprietor and chef of the Huggabie Falls Sanctuary for People Fleeing from Witches and Other Dangerous Flying Creatures, came bursting out of the cafe kitchen, his face as white as a ghost, which is another stupid expression because ghosts are often a murky blue or purple colour, as everyone knows.

He was shaking so much he couldn't speak. He was wheezing and jabbing his finger at the kitchen while he backed away from it.

Kipp jumped up. 'What is it, Froggin? What happened?'

'It's in there,' Froggin said. 'I saw it. It's petrifying. It's a monster.'

Kipp, Tobias and Cymphany stared at each other, as if to say, should we run now and ask questions later? For your information, that is exactly what I would have done if I was in their shoes. Actually, the first thing I would do if I was in their shoes is take them off, because they'd be way too small for me.

Cymphany looked at Froggin, with a look on her face that seemed to say, I don't believe you. 'What sort of monster?' she said.

'The worst kind,' Froggin shrieked. 'It had eight legs.'

'An arachnid?' Cymphany asked.

Arachnid is a fancy word for spider.

'No, a spider,' Froggin said. 'A giant one. Two metres tall. With fangs as big as my legs.'

Tobias straightened up in his seat. 'That's... quite a big spider,' he said. His eyes found the exit door and the street beyond and the big hill beyond that, as if he was calculating whether it would be possible to get to the top of that hill in eight point four seconds.

'Surely there can't be a spider that big,' Cymphany said. 'The maximum recorded height of a spider is only twenty-eight centimetres.'

'*Only?*' Tobias spluttered. 'By the way, on an unrelated topic, how long do you think it would take me to run to the top of that hill out there?'

But Kipp, who was a bit braver than his friend Tobias, or a bit more reckless, said, 'I'll go and check it out. Pass me that broom would you, Froggin?'

Froggin fetched the broom from the corner, and brought it over to Kipp, but Froggin's hands were still shaking so much it took Kipp three grabs to get his hand on it.

'You don't want to go in there, Kipp,' Froggin said. 'I'm not joking. It's the scariest thing I've ever seen.'

'Honestly,' Cymphany said, 'twenty-eight centimetres tall. That's it.'

Kipp smiled. 'The last of the doughnuts are

in there. I'm not letting some giant spider have them all.'

Tobias gulped. 'I'm just going to wait down here,' he stuttered, adopting a sprinter's takeoff pose. 'Just in case.'

Kipp smirked at his friend. 'Very brave, Tobias.'

'What?' Tobias protested. 'I'll get help. When I get to the top of that hill.'

'Be careful,' Cymphany said to Kipp, grinning. She took a toothpick out of her satchel and handed it to him, as if to say, a toothpick will be sufficient defence against whatever kind of spider you're going to find in there.

Kipp politely declined the toothpick. He gripped the broom, and he edged towards the kitchen door. Two pairs of fearful eyes watched from behind him, as well as Cymphany's not-at-all fearful eyes. Actually, there *were* three sets of fearful eyes watching, as, in the opposite corner of the cafe, a tiny spider was peering out from its web in the rafters and wondering if, now that

a two-metre-tall spider had moved into the cafe, it might be time to find another place to live.

Kipp tentatively pushed the door and opened it just a tiny bit. He stuck his head through the gap and looked into the kitchen. What he saw horrified him beyond his wildest nightmares.

2

A Really Short Chapter

Kipp froze, with his body on one side of the door and his head inside the room. 'Oh my,' he managed to say.

'What, what is it?' Tobias asked, lifting his bum in the air and extending his arms—preparing to sprint.

'Is the spider still there?' said Froggin. He was standing on the opposite side of the room with one foot already out the front door.

Cymphany, who had not believed that there

was a two-metre-tall spider in there, held the toothpick out in front of her like a sword.

'It's horrible,' Kipp said. 'It's hideous.'

'What is it?' everyone screamed. If the spider in the corner, who was packing its little spider suitcase at the time, could have talked, it would have shouted, 'Just tell us already. The suspense is killing us.'

And then Kipp unfroze and stepped through the doorway into the kitchen. Everyone else frowned in a mixture of fear and puzzlement.

'It's absolutely revolting,' Kipp shouted back at the others. 'When was the last time you cleaned up in here, Froggin? This kitchen is *filthy*!'

Everyone breathed a sigh of relief—except Froggin. 'It's not that bad,' he said.

'Not that bad?' They could hear Kipp's voice echoing in the kitchen. 'There's mould on top of mould on top of barnacles in here. And this tub of yoghurt sitting on the counter says best before 3 December 1994.'

Tobias and Cymphany gawked at Froggin.

Froggin put his hands up. 'Don't worry. The doughnut-maker is perfectly clean.'

'And what's this doughnut-maker-looking thing covered in green sludge?' they heard Kipp ask. 'Oh, gross! I'm never eating doughnuts here again.'

'Anyway,' said Kipp, as he emerged from the kitchen. 'I can't see any giant spider in there now.' He put the broom back in the corner. 'I think it's gone.'

'But what if it comes back?' Froggin said. 'I'm not going to be here when it does.' He bustled

Kipp, Tobias and Cymphany out the front door, flipped the 'open' sign to 'closed' and stepped out after them. As the door shut behind him he pulled a black marker from his pocket and wrote under the sign on the door: *Permanently!*

'I'm closing the Huggabie Falls Sanctuary for People Fleeing from Witches and Other Dangerous Flying Creatures forever,' Froggin announced, marching away. 'I hate spiders, more than anything. All my life I've been worried about protecting myself from flying creatures, when the scariest monsters are in my own kitchen.'

Froggin dashed across Digmont Drive. Kipp, Tobias and Cymphany barely had time to absorb this turn of events before Mr Yorrick Yugel, manager of the Huggabie Falls bank, rocketed along the footpath from the direction of Digmont Drive, dragging a trolley suitcase, which had various items of clothing poking out of the joins as though it had been packed very hastily.

❖

For those people who are reading this book before the first one (you know who you are, we've talked about this), I'll just quickly explain that every street, road, path, highway, lane and alleyway in Huggabie Falls is named Digmont Drive. No, don't ask me about it. I've said enough already and it's only chapter two.

'Where are you going in such a hurry, Mr Yugel?' Tobias asked.

'And why have you got a hastily packed suitcase with you?' Cymphany asked.

Mr Yugel barely paused. 'There's a shark in my vault.' He looked back fearfully. 'I'm terrified of sharks.'

'A shark?' Cymphany said. 'In a bank vault?'

Mr Yugel nodded, looking like he'd rather continue hurrying than waste time nodding. 'Yes, a pipe burst and the vault filled with water.'

'That may be so,' Cymphany said. 'But it doesn't explain how a shark got in there. I don't believe it.'

'I don't care,' Mr Yugel blurted out. 'I thought the Treacherys not paying their debts was the worst thing I had to worry about in this town'—Tobias shifted uneasily—'but now I've got to deal with a shark! I'm so scared of sharks, I can't stay in Huggabie Falls a moment longer. So I'm shutting down the bank and moving somewhere far away—like the moon. Now, I have to go. There's no point hastily packing your suitcase for a quick getaway, if you then waste time chinwagging.'

Mr Yugel took off so fast that he overtook Froggin, who was still dashing up Digmont Drive, and they both turned right at Digmont Drive and headed towards the Huggabie Falls bus station, on Digmont Drive.

Cymphany, Kipp and Tobias stared at each other. 'Wow,' Kipp said. 'That was all a bit weird...even by Huggabie Falls' particularly weird standards.'

Cymphany shook her head. 'Mr Yugel and Froggin saw things that scared them so much that now the Huggabie Falls bank and the Huggabie Falls Sanctuary for People Fleeing from Witches and other Dangerous Flying Creatures are both shutting down on the same day. Do you know what this means?'

Tobias nodded. 'Yes, it means we're going to have to find a new place to eat doughnuts, and I'll probably never see the money in my junior saver's account ever again. But seeing as I mostly only ever use that money to buy doughnuts, I guess that might not be such a big problem.'

'No,' Kipp said, sharing a look with Cymphany. 'It means a new *thing* is happening in Huggabie Falls.'

'Another one,' Tobias moaned. 'I don't like *things*.'

They all continued to look at each other, with wide eyes and open mouths, until Cymphany said, 'You know who we have to talk to?'

Kipp and Tobias nodded. They all knew exactly who they had to talk to.

Two Extremely Difficult Smiles

Those people who have read the first book in the Huggabie Falls trilogy, will already know that Kipp, Tobias and Cymphany always went to see Mr Haurik when they had an important question, or when they needed advice or guidance.

Mr Harold Haurik was a wise old man who claimed to hate pirates, yet he had a wooden leg, an eye patch and a parrot, and he always spoke in just the way you'd imagine a pirate would talk.

He used to live on the shore of the bottomless lake in a four-storey caravan, which, among other features, had a swimming pool, three hot-tub spa baths and a rooftop tennis court. But then he installed that caravan into a pirate ship so he could sail it across the lake.

(~~Honestly, this is getting beyond a joke. I wouldn't have to explain all this if the non-first-book readers weren't still here. Surely you should have learnt your lesson by now. Just go and read the first book, will you, please. I mean, do us all a favour!~~ *Comments deleted by the publisher, and author warned to behave nicely to all readers, because all readers are wonderful people, and some readers might have a very good reason why they haven't read the first book in the Huggabie Falls trilogy.*)

Mr Haurik used to come ashore often,

until the local council banned cutlasses on the lakefront. Now he spent all his time sailing the bottomless lake. So the only way Kipp, Tobias and Cymphany could communicate with him was through smoke signals from a campfire on the shore, which was both extremely time consuming and extremely dangerous.

On the day the scary things happened to Mr Yugel and Froggin, Kipp, Tobias and Cymphany needed to ask Mr Haurik some questions, but they didn't have time to build a fire and ruin another school jumper by making the smoke signals.

So they went to see another adult who they thought could help them, because this adult seemed to know about everything that happened in Huggabie Falls. That adult was Felonious Dark. His agency on Digmont Drive used to be called Dark's Weirdness Investigation and Eradication Agency, but it had recently been renamed: The Felonious Dark (Reformed Evil-Doer) Non-Evil Promotions Agency.

Readers who have read the first Huggabie Falls book, also known as my favourite people, will be a bit confused now, because they will remember that Felonious Dark was a tall, thin, evil man who, along with a creepy scientist, was responsible for the extremely weird thing that happened in Huggabie Falls, and that he also once tried to feed Kipp, Tobias and Cymphany to vegetarian piranhas. So you're probably wondering why Kipp, Tobias and Cymphany were going to see Felonious Dark for advice.

Well, as per Felonious Dark's newly named agency, he was a reformed evil-doer, which means he no longer did evil things like sneaking into supermarkets after dark and swapping all the strawberry-jam labels with the labels for Señor Firebreather's Super-Hot Chilli Paste.

Now, when I first heard that Kipp, Tobias and Cymphany were trusting Felonious Dark, I thought, oh dear, that's a shame, these children will soon meet a grisly end and I will have to find three other children to write this book about. But it did seem that Felonious Dark was, mostly, or at least nearly almost, reformed.

Kipp, Tobias and Cymphany entered the waiting room of Felonious Dark's agency, which was still drafty and still had the same uncomfortable little steel chairs in the waiting room and the same large receptionist with the same purple curlers in her same red hair, but now, to show the agency was reformed, it had a welcome mat on the floor in the doorway, or, to be more precise, it had a welcome mat still in its box by the doorway.

The receptionist looked up and grunted when they walked in. 'Go away,' she snarled.

'Gertrude,' they heard Felonious Dark call out sternly from the room next door. 'Remember what we practised.'

The receptionist sighed and took a deep breath. Then she began to strain and grimace with considerable effort, like she was trying to open a very tight jar of pickles. She winced as she stretched her mouth open, driving her cheek muscles back towards her ears, then slightly up, and inch by inch she prised her mouth open until she was exposing two tightly clenched rows of yellow teeth. As she held this pose, her eyeballs bulged and beads of sweat trickled down her face.

Cymphany leaned over to Kipp and Tobias and whispered, 'Is she trying to smile?'

'I think so,' Kipp said, with an expression of disgust mixed with a little bit of fear on his face.

Tobias's face went even more white than usual. 'That's the most disturbing thing I've ever seen,' he said.

Felonious Dark appeared in the doorway. 'Very good, Gertrude,' he said. 'Excellent progress. Children, a pleasure as always. Come in.'

As Kipp, Tobias and Cymphany entered Felonious Dark's office, they heard the sound of a great expulsion of air behind them, followed by the sound of Gertrude slumping forward and collapsing on her desk.

'Welcome to the Felonious Dark (Reformed Evil-Doer) Non-Evil Promotions Agency,' said Felonious Dark as he swept his arms around the room, as if to show how reformed the entire office was. 'Reformed evil-doer,' he repeated, and he held up one finger. 'Emphasis on the *reformed*.'

'Hi, Mr Dark,' Kipp, Tobias and Cymphany said at the same time.

Felonious Dark shook their hands in turn.

'How's the non-evilness going, Mr Dark?' Cymphany asked.

Felonious Dark's face darkened. 'Very well, thank you.'

Tobias's arm jerked, and he looked at his wrist. 'Mr Dark, did you just steal my watch?'

Felonious Dark looked guilty. 'Sorry,' he said, and he pulled Tobias's watch from his pocket and handed it back to him. 'It's not easy giving up evil-doing, but I'm trying my hardest.'

Kipp, Tobias and Cymphany sat in the chairs in front of Felonious Dark's desk, in the gloomy candlelit office. Felonious Dark had tried to brighten the room up and make it less ominous by putting a flower on his desk, but the flower looked like it had died quite some time ago. He had also purchased a giant pet lizard, since the children had last visited, which sat on his lap.

'What have you come to see me about, children?' Felonious Dark reclined in his chair and patted his giant pet lizard.

The lizard hissed at Kipp, Tobias and Cymphany and they all jumped, but then Felonious Dark snapped, 'Hissy. No! Remember what we talked about.' And then the lizard did the same thing that Gertrude had done a few minutes ago: with great strain, it stretched its green cheek muscles back and up to expose two rows of clenched teeth. It was very unsettling for Kipp, Tobias and Cymphany to watch a lizard try to smile like this.

'You were saying, kids?' Felonious Dark said, urging them to continue.

So Cymphany, Kipp and Tobias ignored the

weirdly smiling lizard and told Felonious Dark about Froggin and the unbelievably scary spider he saw in his kitchen, and Mr Yugel and the equally unbelievable and equally scary shark in his vault. And about how they had both closed their establishments and left town immediately, and how it was quite a coincidence that both these seemingly unrelated unbelievably scary things happened at the same time, so maybe they actually were related.

Felonious Dark listened and looked thoughtful as they spoke, and when they were finished he stopped patting his pet lizard, whose face skin had changed from green to red, and who now had little beads of sweat rolling down its tiny lizard forehead as it strained to hold its smile. Felonious Dark stood up and walked to the wall and stared at it.

'You know,' he said after a few moments. 'I really need to get a window installed here. It would be great for staring out of.'

Kipp, Tobias and Cymphany waited. 'Well,

Mr Dark?' Tobias said at last. 'What do you think?'

Felonious Dark turned back from the wall. 'It's all quite unbelievable, I hardly believe it myself. But it sounds like someone is up to no good. Up to evil-doings, as it were. And usually people contact me if they want some evil-doings done, as not everyone knows I am reformed yet. I find it hard to believe that no one has contacted me...' Felonious Dark twiddled his moustache. 'Hmmmm...I wonder, if it could be...'

Cymphany looked at Kipp and Tobias and then said what they were all thinking. 'What, Mr Dark? What do you wonder?'

'There is someone else.' He let go of his moustache. 'Not quite as evil as I am...errr...I mean, not quite as evil as I once was, but still very high on the evil-ability scale. I haven't seen him for a long time...but maybe...just maybe, he might be back.'

Kipp looked urgently at Cymphany and Tobias, as if to say, do you want me to be the one who says what we are all thinking this time? He took their return looks to mean yes, go ahead, and he said, 'Who, Mr Dark? Who?'

Felonious Dark turned and opened his mouth to say something, but before he could answer, Gertrude burst into the room.

'It's horrible,' she screamed. 'It's in the town square. It's the scariest thing you've ever seen.' And she bolted from the office, through the waiting room, and out the front door.

Felonious Dark, Kipp, Tobias and Cymphany stood there for a millisecond, and then they all ran out the front door as well.

Not one of them heard the sound behind them of a mini expulsion of air followed by the sound of a lizard slumping forward and collapsing onto a desk.

4

Why Inside a Portaloo Is Not a Great Place to Hide

Kipp, Tobias, Cymphany and Felonious Dark raced after Gertrude into the town square to be confronted by a Tyrannosaurus Rex, a skyscraper of a dinosaur with very small arms but very big teeth, which meant it was destined to be very bad at basketball but potentially very good at biting things in half. Biting something in half was actually what it was doing as Kipp, Tobias, Cymphany and Felonious Dark ran into the square.

'Is that our school bus?' Cymphany asked as she skidded to a stop.

'That's half of it.' Kipp pointed. 'The other half is flying off over there.'

Tobias gulped. 'I hope there were no children on board.'

Felonious Dark shook his head. 'The school bus is being rented by the DFA today, the Dinosaur Fearers Anonymous group, for one of their field trips.'

In any normal situation, I'm sure Kipp, Cymphany and Tobias would have stared in wonder at Felonious Dark, as if to say how could you possibly know that? I am certainly wondering myself. But they were too busy watching the dinosaur swish its giant tail into the Huggabie Falls Demolition Services building, demolishing it, which was hilariously ironic, but any humour in the situation was completely lost on the Huggabie Falls DFA members, who were too busy screaming, flailing their arms and running for their lives. Many of them were wearing white shirts with the DFA logo on them: a dinosaur inside a red circle with a red line across it. Funnily enough, the dinosaur pictured in the logo was a brontosaurus, a non-meat-eating and non-threatening kind of dinosaur. Surely a dangerous Tyrannosaurus Rex, a T-Rex, like the one rampaging through town at that very moment, would have been a more appropriate dinosaur to have on their logo. Considering many members of the DFA were currently being picked up, flung into the air and swallowed whole by a T-Rex, that change would more than likely be proposed at their next general meeting, if there were any members of the DFA left to attend that meeting.

As Kipp, Tobias, Cymphany, Felonious Dark and Gertrude watched the T-Rex carnage, with the same look of horror on their faces as someone might have if they've just found out the world had run out of marmalade, something unexpected happened. The T-Rex stopped, mid-smashing-tail-swing, and sniffed the air.

Then it turned its head and locked its eyes on Kipp, Tobias, Cymphany, Felonious Dark and Gertrude. It sniffed the air again. Its eyes bulged, its jaw dropped, and a glob of saliva dribbled from its open mouth.

It's commonly thought that T-Rex's have bad eyesight and can only see something if it moves. I'm no dinosaur expert, but that is an easy opinion to have when a T-Rex is not staring at you in the same way a starving man, trapped on a desert island, who has not eaten in weeks, might stare at a passing ship with a fried-chicken logo on the side.

Kipp, Tobias, Cymphany and Gertrude looked terrified. The only person who didn't look terrified was Felonious Dark, because he was too busy looking guilty.

'Now might be a good time,' Felonious Dark gulped, 'to mention that I have a piece of beef jerky in my pocket.'

Tobias looked at him. 'I was wondering what that smell was.'

35

'Okay,' Kipp said calmly. 'No one panic. We'll be okay just as long as we don't make any sudden move—'

'Run!' Gertrude screamed, and she turned and sprinted down Digmont Drive.

So that pretty much destroyed Kipp's not-panicking plans. They ran down Digmont Drive and turned into Digmont Drive. Under them, the ground shuddered, and behind them huge thudding dinosaur feet pounded the earth.

Kipp caught up to Felonious Dark. 'Why don't you throw the beef jerky behind us, and maybe the T-Rex will stop and eat it?'

Felonious Dark shook his head as he ran, his arms pumping like pistons. 'I have a sneaky suspicion that won't work,' he said between panting breaths.

'Why is that?' Cymphany screamed over the deafening dinosaur roar, which sounded like it was getting closer behind them.

'Because,' Felonious Dark said, 'I did that about a hundred metres ago and the T-Rex is

still chasing us.'

Cymphany shook her head. 'This is ridiculous. What are we running away from? Dinosaurs don't exist—they've been extinct for sixty-five million years. There is no way that this is actually happening.'

Tobias shrugged, which is hard to do when you're running full pelt. 'Maybe this one didn't die out. Maybe it was sleeping.'

Cymphany glared at Tobias, which is also hard to do while you are running full pelt. 'Asleep for sixty-five million years?'

'Sure,' Tobias said. 'Once when I was really tired, I slept in till three-thirty in the afternoon.'

'Tobias, I'm not having this conversation anymore,' Cymphany said.

And at that exact moment, Kipp said, 'Down here,' and he ducked into an alley.

Cymphany, Tobias, Felonious Dark and Gertrude ducked right in behind him, just as the T-Rex thundered past.

Then the thundering stopped, and was

replaced by a lot of crashing, and tail-bashing, which all sounded suspiciously like a Tyrannosaurus Rex doing a U-turn.

'It will be back in a second,' Felonious Dark said. 'Thirteen actually. Tyrannosaurus Rexes take exactly thirteen seconds to do a U-turn.'

Again, if Kipp, Tobias and Cymphany had had more time they would have asked Felonious Dark how he could possibly know that obscure fact. But they didn't have time, so Tobias just said the most completely obvious thing ever recorded as being said in human history: 'We need to find a hiding spot.'

But the alley was a dead end, and all that was at the end of the alley was a sign for Huggabie Falls Pet Insurance, with a slogan under it that read:

No Pet Too Small, No Pet Too Big.

Again, the hilarious irony of this sign was lost on everyone in the alley. What wasn't lost on Kipp, Tobias, Cymphany, Felonious Dark and

Gertrude was a line of five blue portable toilets, portaloos. Kipp looked down the line of people. There were five of them. He looked back at the five portaloos. 'Are you guys thinking what I'm thinking?' he said.

A few seconds later, Cymphany sat crouched on a toilet inside one of the five blue plastic portaloos. It was quiet. Some would say too quiet, but then again what is too quiet? Quiet is just quiet.

'Cymphany?' she heard Kipp's voice, and she looked confused, seemingly because his voice didn't sound all echoey like she would have expected it to sound if Kipp was in one of the other four portaloos.

'Yes, Kipp?' Cymphany replied, and she jumped with surprise at how echoey her voice was inside the portaloo.

'Why aren't you hiding under the sign like the rest of us?' Kipp asked.

Cymphany frowned. '*That* was what you were thinking!'

'Of course,' Kipp said. 'To trick the dinosaur into thinking we were hiding in the portaloos, then hoping it would eat the portaloos, and maybe it wouldn't like the taste of blue plastic, and it would run away.'

'Right,' said Cymphany slowly.

'I thought,' Kipp said, even more slowly, 'you knew what I was thinking.'

Cymphany frowned again. It was what she did best. 'As if anyone could know you were thinking that!'

'I knew,' Tobias said. And Cymphany's face screwed up, as she made a mental note to have a stern talk with Tobias later.

'I knew too,' Felonious Dark said.

And then, a few seconds later, a third voice, Gertrude's, said, 'Actually, I didn't know—I just followed Mr Dark.'

Cymphany rolled her eyes. 'It doesn't matter: I can't hear it, so it must have gone. And, besides, like I said earlier'—she spoke like someone who puts a lot of faith in what they've read in textbooks—'dinosaurs are extinct. There is no way there's a Tyrannosaurus Rex out there. It's not possible.'

At that exact moment there was a thundering roar and two giant teeth speared through the plastic of the portaloo. Cymphany reeled, presumably alarmed at the rather unpleasant, stomach-flipping sensation of the portaloo being lifted into the air and the door, which she had forgotten to lock, swinging open.

Kipp, who had crawled out from under the sign, found himself staring up at Cymphany, who was clutching onto and dangling from a toilet-roll holder. She looked down at Kipp in shock. 'Either you just got a lot smaller,' she said, 'or I just got a lot higher.'

The Tyrannosaurus Rex, who had the portaloo with Cymphany inside it in its jaws, threw back its head, flipping Cymphany back inside the blue plastic portaloo.

The dinosaur spread its stance, swung its head again and roared as it clamped its jaws down on the portaloo, which began to splinter and buckle.

'Cymphany!' Tobias screamed. 'Jump. I'll catch you.'

Cymphany smiled, as though she didn't want to hurt her friend's feelings. 'No, thank you,' she said, as if to say, the only thing Tobias was really good at catching was colds.

As the dinosaur's jaw clenching continued, a plastic shard snapped off the side of the portaloo and the roof started to crumple.

'We'll all catch you,' Kipp said, looking back to Felonious Dark and Gertrude, only to find they were about fifty metres away, running back down the alley.

'Sorry,' Felonious Dark called back. 'I'm mostly reformed, but I'm still working on building up positive character traits like bravery and helping others. You could say I'm a bit of a work in prog—'

At that point Felonious Dark and Gertrude disappeared around the corner, and you couldn't

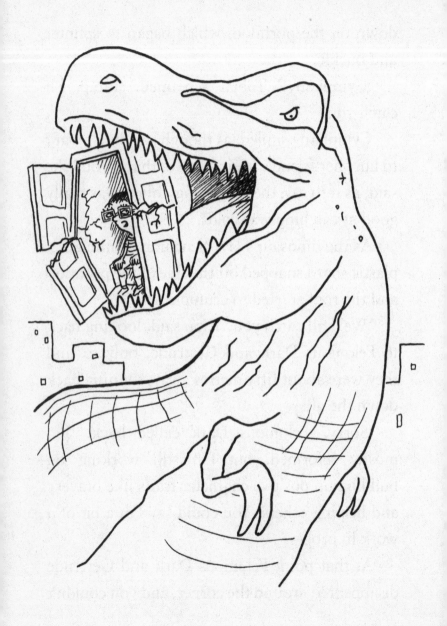

catch the end of the sentence, but I'm going to take a wild guess that it was '*ress*'.

'Okay, then,' Kipp said, as he turned back to look up at Cymphany. 'Tobias and I will catch you.'

Tobias nodded, in a less-than-confident-but-willing-to-give-it-a-try-to-save-my-friend manner.

Cymphany shook her head. 'It's okay. I'm fine. As I've told you already, dinosaurs don't exist.' She didn't seem to notice a faint voice, coming from the deep recesses of the dinosaur's open mouth. 'Help, we're members of the Dinosaur Fearer's Anonymous group, and we've been swallowed whole and are currently inside a dinosaur's belly, which, due to our particular phobias, is entirely the last place we want to be right now. If you could be so kind as to throw a rope down, that would be great, but if not, please pass on our feedback to the DFA committee that, all things considered, this has not been one of the DFA's best field trips.'

But Cymphany didn't hear this noise over the straining and buckling of the plastic of the portaloo and Kipp screaming from the ground, 'Dinosaurs do exist, Cymph. One is about to eat you, so hurry up and get out of there would you?'

At this point in the story you might be getting a little bit scared that one of the main characters is about to get eaten by a dinosaur. You're probably thinking, I should have known something like this was going to happen, as this book is called *The Unbelievably Scary Thing that Happened in Huggabie Falls*, but I had no idea it was going to be this unbelievable. I had no idea a main character was going to get eaten by a dinosaur, in a portaloo of all places!

As the author of this book, I was worried that this scene might cause undue distress to readers, and it's for this reason that I did suggest to my publisher that a sticker be put on the cover of the book warning readers that characters, both minor and major, in this book might be eaten by dinosaurs. But my publisher thought this might spoil the suspense of the story. And who wants to read a book when they already know what is going to happen? Personally, I think that if I saw a shopful of books and one of them had a sticker on the front warning that characters inside could be eaten by dinosaurs, that would be the first book I would pick up.

But it is distressing when a major character is about to be eaten, especially if that character is Cymphany Chan. I notice no one seemed concerned for the various members of the Dinosaur Fearers Anonymous group, who, as we heard moments ago, had already been swallowed. It's hardly surprising. People rarely care about the fate of nameless characters. It may interest you to know that one of those characters, Truman Trotter, who was actually the DFA member trying to call out to Cymphany, is one minor character that I had actually planned to make into a major character in a future book, so I personally was very upset to find out that he got swallowed. I'm not so sure he will make it to a future book now. I mean perhaps those swallowed characters will all band together and formulate an escape plan, but I have to say their odds of survival are poor—and that's being optimistic.

Anyway, where was I? Oh yes, Cymphany, still refusing to believe it was possible she was about to be eaten by an extinct creature, heard the plastic of the portaloo squealing and buckling, which lasted only a second, before the portaloo's frame gave way and the dinosaur clamped its jaws shut.

5

I Hope This Is Not
a New Chapter

I am not a fan of the practice of ending a chapter on a cliffhanger, where, say—hypothetically speaking—a major character in a portaloo is in the process of being bitten in half by a dinosaur. These sorts of shameless, suspense-building techniques might be great for building tension, but they are very distressing for characters inside portaloos that are being bitten in half by dinosaurs. This is why I did not end this chapter right as Cymphany was being eaten by the T-Rex.

But, just in case the publisher inserted a chapter break just as Cymphany was being eaten, I sincerely apologise. I do not condone behaviour like this, and all letters of complaint should be addressed directly to the publisher, as I cannot handle any more letters—since writing *The Extremely Weird Thing that Happened in Huggabie Falls* my letterbox is full to bursting with fan mail, as you'd expect.

Now we have that out of the way, I know you are dying to find out what happened to Cymphany, so I shall get on with the story without any more pesky, unnecessary, supposedly suspense-building chapter breaks.

6

Oh, This Is Getting Ridiculous

So without further ado (another silly expression, because why would anyone possibly add *ado* to anything. I don't even know what *ado* is, but I imagine the last thing anyone ever wants is further of it), here is what happened to Cymphany.

When the portaloo was bitten in two, the only thing that stopped Cymphany from instantly being bitten in two too, was her ability to crouch down lower than the height of the portaloo's toilet.

This small porcelain toilet withstood the crushing force of the dinosaur's bite admirably, and kept the portaloo from flattening completely. But it wasn't a very strong porcelain toilet and it soon turned into a spiderweb of stress cracks and looked like it too was about to collapse.

When Cymphany realised she was about to end up in a similar condition to one of the chicken drumsticks she ate last night, she had about one second to think, perhaps I should rethink this whole extinct-animals-don't-exist idea now that I'm about to be eaten by one— what textbook did I even read that sixty-five-million-years thing in anyway?—before the screeching and plastic splitting sound suddenly stopped.

Cymphany watched the world swivel, and then, through a narrow gap between the dinosaur's clamped-together teeth, she saw a person standing on top of a tall building eye-to-eye with the T-Rex.

It was Gertrude.

The dinosaur snorted air through its nostrils, which blew Gertrude's hair backwards, and the dinosaur glared at her, as if to say, what do you think you're doing standing on the top of a tall building and looking me in the eye? I am in the middle of crushing this portaloo, and I'm not sure I like you watching.

Gertrude didn't move, and this seemed to confuse the T-Rex, who was obviously more accustomed to people turning and running away in fear than just standing and staring with their arms crossed. The T-Rex looked perplexed, which is a very hard look to pull off when you don't have any eyebrows.

Gertrude dropped her arms and took a deep breath. And then her face twisted. She grunted and strained, and her face turned purple with agonised effort. Millimetre by millimetre, her cheek muscles played tug of war with the edges of her lips, finally dragging them out towards her ears, and then her ear muscles took over and forced the edges of her lips upwards, while at the same time her lips wrenched apart to expose two fiercely clenched rows of teeth. She held this pained expression for what seemed like an eternity, until her eyeballs looked ready to pop out of their sockets and bounce across the rooftops.

The dinosaur watched her. And then its eyes widened, and it roared. It let go of the almost-completely-flattened portaloo and then it turned and stomped back down the alley—not stopping or even looking back, as it ploughed through ten buildings in a row. And it kept going until it finally disappeared somewhere near the horizon.

Cymphany rolled out of the portaloo, and Kipp and Tobias ran over to her. They all looked up at the tall building.

With the dinosaur gone, Gertrude released the smile from her face, accompanied by a gigantic expulsion of air. Then she staggered, her eyes rolled backwards into her head, and she collapsed onto the rooftop.

Fortuitous Flyers

If something advantageous happens at just the right moment, it is said to be fortuitous. For example, it was fortuitous that at the exact moment Cymphany was about to find out what being chomped in two felt like, Gertrude appeared on that rooftop and scared the dinosaur away with her smile.

Hours after this fortuitous event, Cymphany was at home, lying in her bed and thinking she might change her opinion from dinosaurs definitely *are* extinct to dinosaurs definitely *should be* extinct.

And as Kipp lay in bed that night he decided that next time he asked people if they were thinking what he was thinking, he might just say what he was thinking instead, to avoid any confusion.

And Tobias was thinking, wow, all this stuff that is going on really is *unbelievably* scary. I'm glad I've got a night light.

Cymphany, Kipp and Tobias had finally gone home after spending the afternoon discussing the fortuitous timing of Gertrude's appearance on the rooftop, as well as the unbelievably scary things that were happening all over Huggabie Falls and how none of them had the foggiest idea what was causing them all.

The next day, on the way to school, another fortuitous thing happened—this time to Kipp. A brochure fluttering along on this windless day flew up and slapped Kipp in the face. Now this alone does not sound fortuitous, I know. In fact, it sounds a little bit more like a for-crying-out-loud-ious moment. And Kipp certainly didn't think it was fortuitous at the time.

In fact the first thing he thought was: *Hang on, are we in the middle of a solar eclipse, because the world has gone dark all of a sudden...oh, wait, it's just a piece of paper on my face.*

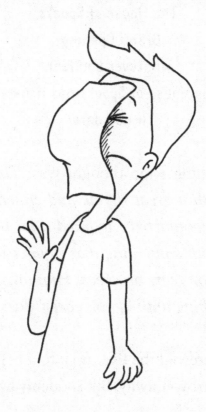

He pulled the piece of paper off his face and noticed it was a flyer, both in terms of the fact it was flying through the air and also that it was a piece of paper with advertising material printed on it, otherwise known as a flyer:

New Huggabie Falls Attraction
The House of Spooks
Grand Opening!
Whatever you fear,
The House of Spooks has it here,
If you dare.

The first thing Kipp thought was: *That slogan started with a great rhyme and ended with no rhyme. It would have worked a lot better if it finished with something that rhymes with here, like deer, or rear, or cheer. Hmmm...but then again finishing with 'if you cheer' doesn't sound scary at all.*

Kipp screwed the flyer up into a ball and was about to throw it away. But suddenly he thought:

Hang on a second.

Now I wish Kipp had thought, hang on a second, I'd better not litter, because littering is wrong—it's very bad for the environment. I'd better put this bit of paper safely in my pocket until I find a rubbish bin. But he wasn't thinking that, which is a sign that Huggabie Falls Primary School really needs to step up its anti-littering program. In case you're wondering, its anti-littering slogan was:

Keep the Streets Clean
and Serene.
It's a Good Thing to Do.

Coincidentally, Huggabie Falls Primary School employed the same marketing company for its anti-litter program that the House of Spooks employed for its grand opening event, a marketing company that was great at making their slogans start with the perfect rhyme, but not great at making their slogans finish with one.

But Kipp wasn't thinking about the evils of littering, or bad rhyming slogans. He was thinking about the amazing coincidence that at the same time that Huggabie Falls residents were being terrified by unbelievably scary things, a place called the House of Spooks was opening.

It was also weird that the only way he had found out about the House of Spooks was that on a completely still, windless day a flyer had blown into his face.

Kipp frowned as he unscrewed the flyer. 'Well,' he said. 'That was fortuitous.'

And that is exactly what it was: fortuitous. As soon as I found out that this had happened to Kipp, I thought, I hope the readers at home (or on buses, or on horseback, or in the middle of a fencing contest—or wherever you are) don't think that this is another conveniently placed clue. In the first book of the Huggabie Falls trilogy, a business card turned up in the letterbox of Kipp Kindle's house, which led Kipp, Tobias and Cymphany to Felonious Dark's agency. It was an extremely helpful business card, and as such readers had the audacity to accuse me of planting it in the letterbox.

As I explained then, and as I am pained to explain again, I have no control over what happens in this story or what turns up in letterboxes or blows into faces. I am not able to control the actions of the characters in this story, like some devilishly handsome puppet-master. I am merely recounting the events of this story, exactly as they happened.

So I was as surprised by the fortuitous flyer as Cymphany and Tobias were when Kipp showed it to them at school a little later that day.

'Wow,' said Tobias, holding the flyer in his hands. 'That slogan would really work a lot better if it ended with a rhyme.'

Kipp smiled. 'I thought exactly the same thing.'

'You're both missing the point,' Cymphany said, with the tone of someone who always gets the point and loves pointing out when others are missing it. 'The House of Spooks has obviously got something to do with all the unbelievably scary things happening in Huggabie Falls.'

'What happened to that dinosaur?' Tobias asked, glancing nervously outside. 'You don't think it will come back, do you?'

Cymphany shook her head. 'Last I heard the authorities were chasing it up the topless hill, and as that hill has no top, they could be chasing it for quite some time. Meanwhile, the members of the DFA, the ones who weren't eaten, have all left town.'

'I don't blame them,' Kipp said. 'I heard they also changed their logo to one that features a Tyrannosaurus Rex, which I think we all saw coming.'

'Who do you think is going to be scared next?' Tobias wondered aloud.

With impeccable timing, Mrs Turgan burst into class a moment later, screaming, *Bathtubs*.'

Mrs Turgan often came into class screaming

things, usually spells that resulted in children getting turned into newts, or complaints that the prices of cauldrons were going up again even though they were 'sky high' already. But she had never come in screaming 'bathtubs' before.

She slammed the door shut and leaned a chair against the handle so that the door was wedged shut. Then she ran across the room and flung herself behind her desk.

Kipp, Tobias and Cymphany, and Ug Ugg—who was sitting in front of them and who was not a child but a troll—looked at each other.

Mrs Turgan peeked out from behind her desk, trembling. She fixed her eyes on the door.

Ug Ugg raised his hand. 'Is something the matter, Mrs Turgan?' he asked. 'And will it have any impact on our maths test today?'

The rest of the class groaned. Ug Ugg was the only student who actually enjoyed maths tests.

But Mrs Turgan didn't seem to hear Ug. She mumbled, 'Bathtubs. Bathtubs. They're chasing me everywhere. They've even got...'

She gulped. 'Rubber duckies in them.'

Cymphany glanced at Tobias and Kipp, as if to say, I think we just answered the question of who is going to be unbelievably scared next. She put up her hand. 'Mrs Turgan, you haven't been anywhere near the House of Spooks, have you?'

This seemed to get Mrs Turgan's attention. 'Why would I go there?' she snapped. 'Although, come to think of it, I was walking past that new House of Spooks place when the first bathtub started to chase me. I haven't had a bath since 1951, and I don't intend to have another one anytime soon. They make you smell like'—she shuddered—'lavender.'

There was a creaking noise in the hallway

outside, and the sound of sloshing water. Mrs Turgan shrieked. She pointed her wand at the top of her head with one hand and opened her desk drawer with the other. 'I'm going to turn myself into a pencil sharpener and hide in this drawer,' she wailed, and then she blurted out something that Kipp, Tobias and Cymphany couldn't quite understand, but it definitely had the words 'hocus pocus' in it. A green spark flew from the tip of her wand, and there was flash of light. Mrs Turgan disappeared, leaving only the sound of plastic tinkling on wood, which was presumably the sound of a pencil sharpener falling into the drawer.

The class went completely silent. There was another creak in the hallway, followed by a slosh, and all the students turned and stared expectantly through the window in the classroom door. A moment later Huggabie Falls Primary School specialist science teacher Mr Dungolly strolled past, swishing coffee in his coffee cup. He took a loud slurp of his coffee, which echoed in the silent hallway, and plodded off. He wasn't a bathtub. It seemed Mrs Turgan's fears were unfounded. But Mrs Turgan wouldn't have worked this out, as pencil sharpeners don't have eyes or ears or brains.

Ug Ugg put up a timid hand. 'Is that a no to the maths test, Mrs Turgan?'

Kipp, Tobias and Cymphany looked at each other. 'Are you both thinking what I'm thinking?' Kipp asked.

Cymphany and Tobias nodded. 'That we should definitely visit the House of Spooks after school?' Cymphany suggested.

'Oh good,' Kipp smiled. 'This time you actually *were* thinking what I was thinking. We're obviously all getting a lot better at this.'

So, after school Kipp, Tobias and Cymphany went to check out the House of Spooks, which they only knew about thanks to the fortuitous flyer that had been blown by an invisible wind. The flyer also indicated that the House of

Spooks address was 1884 Digmont Drive. As we've already established, a place's address in Huggabie Falls is no help in finding that place, due to the fact that every street in Huggabie Falls is called Digmont Drive. But Kipp, Tobias and Cymphany were able to narrow down their search area somewhat, as they were quite familiar with many parts of Huggabie Falls, especially those near sweets shops or video game arcades, and they probably would have noticed if those parts had suddenly acquired a new attraction called the House of Spooks.

Now at this point in the story, I should probably address the fact that many readers would have screwed their noses up when they read that Huggabie Falls had sweets shops and video game arcades. I understand that many children may not even be aware of what a video arcade is. Most children these days carry video game arcades around in their pockets on mobile phones, which seem to be able to do everything.

I saw a child the other day using a mobile phone to order a pizza, which I found quite impressive, especially as we were in the International Space Station at the time.

Anyway, in Huggabie Falls things are, as we already know, weird. One of the weird things about Huggabie Falls is that it is very dangerous to carry a mini-computer, like a mobile phone, around with you, on account of the fact that computer viruses in Huggabie Falls are not standard computer viruses, but weird ones that like to also infect people. In Huggabie Falls, if you catch a computer virus your mind starts to get corrupted. Like the time Henrietta Humpling's father suddenly started believing he was a chicken, and he stuck feathers all over his body and moved into the neighbour's chicken coop. The only way to get rid of these weird Huggabie Falls computer–human viruses is to pay for a computer–human-virus removalist to come around and reboot you, which doesn't mean they give you a new pair of boots. It means they reset your mind, back to some time before you caught the virus, which could end up being when you were a baby, which would mean you would have to relearn everything you've ever learnt in your entire life all over again. And sometimes, even then, the virus never totally goes away. To this day, Mr Humpling still wakes up some mornings and is alarmed to find a freshly laid egg in his bed.

So, considering the dangers of computers in Huggabie Falls, it was very surprising to Kipp, Tobias and Cymphany, when they walked along the Digmont Drive that winds up the hill beside town—hoping that they could see the House of Spooks from up there—that they found Felonious Dark talking on a mobile phone.

Felonious Dark smiled suspiciously as they walked up to him, and said, 'I'll call you back,' into the phone, and then popped it in his trousers pocket.

'Mr Dark,' Cymphany said in alarm. 'Aren't you worried about catching a computer virus?

My mum caught one once and she got corrupted: she started drinking tomato sauce straight from the bottle—it was horrible.'

Felonious Dark smiled. 'It's all right. It's not even on. I just like to pretend I'm talking on a mobile phone so that I look important.'

Tobias chuckled. 'Mr Dark, if you keep doing weird things like that, you're going to become a typical Huggabie Falls resident in no time.'

'What are you even doing up here, Mr Dark?' Kipp asked.

'I'm trying to find the House of Spooks,' Felonious Dark said, removing a flyer from his pocket. 'I've been wondering about all the unbelievably scary things that keep happening, and then this flyer blew into my face this morning, even though there wasn't a breath of wind about. It was quite—'

'Fortuitous?' Tobias interrupted.

'I was going to say annoying,' Felonious Dark said. 'But fortuitous will do.'

Kipp exclaimed that a flyer had blown into

his face that extremely calm, unwindy morning as well.

'It's almost,' Cymphany said, 'as if some invisible force is controlling this world we live in, and dropping convenient clues on us right when we need them; I mean, remember the business card in the letterbox when we were trying to find out about the extremely weird thing that happened in Huggabie Falls?'

I honestly can't believe Cymphany said that. I mean here I am trying to convince you that I am not manipulating this story by planting flyers, or business cards, for that matter, and Cymphany goes and says something potentially reputation-ruining like that. I tell you, my life would be a lot easier if I just wrote nice fictional characters, who said nice fictional things I could control. But I don't, so let's just get on with it.

And by the way, did you believe what Felonious Dark said about his mobile phone not being turned on? If you did, then perhaps you need to think a bit about who you are trusting in this story. Especially since the hill beside Huggabie Falls is one of the best places in Huggabie Falls to get a mobile phone signal.

Kipp, like me, didn't believe that Felonious Dark's mobile phone wasn't turned on, especially because Felonious Dark's pocket kept vibrating as he and the children walked up to the highest point of the hill. On the other side of the hill Digmont Drive ran down to the Digmont Drive that crossed the Huggabie Falls River and was the only road out of town.

From the top of the hill they could see all of Huggabie Falls spread out beneath them, including the far off misty lake, which was full of vegetarian piranhas and had a water treatment plant in the middle, which was where Kipp, Tobias and Cymphany had succeeded in foiling the creepy scientist's plans. They could also see all the way from the dam walls of the hydro-electric power station on one side of town to the dam walls of the hydro-electric power station on the other side of town. One of the weird things about Huggabie Falls—of which, as you know, there were many—was the fact that there was a hydro-electric power station on each side of town. This made it a particularly bad idea to arrange to meet someone by the hydro-electric power station, because if you went to the wrong one, you'd be as far away from meeting that person as you could possibly be.

Kipp, Tobias, Cymphany and Felonious Dark stood on the top of the hill and looked at the town below. Cymphany took a telescope out of her satchel and extended it. Did I mention that Cymphany always

carried a satchel that seemed to have a useful item in it for any occasion? I wouldn't even have to mention it if those people who hadn't read the first book had quickly raced off and read it in between chapters one and two. Don't even get me started.

Felonious Dark raised an eyebrow. 'You carry a telescope around with you?' he said questioningly.

Cymphany shrugged. 'Yes. It pays to be prepared.' Cymphany put the telescope to her eye and began to sweep it slowly back and forth over the town.

Tobias shook his head. 'Why does Huggabie Falls need two hydro-electric plants, anyway? We're only a small town.'

'There,' Cymphany said, pointing. 'I see a tall wonky old house, with black clouds above it and vultures circling the spires.'

Kipp squinted and strained, because he didn't have the telescope. 'That's definitely the place. Down there, on the north side of Digmont Drive.'

'Actually'—Tobias put his finger up—'it's on the south side of Digmont Drive. What you're looking at is the reflection of the House of Spooks in the Huggabie Falls Mirror Emporium on the other side of the road.'

'Wow'—Cymphany adjusted the focus on her telescope—'that's a *huge* mirror.'

Felonious Dark clapped his hands together. 'Well, what are we waiting for. Let's get down there.'

Kipp raised an eyebrow as he looked at Felonious Dark. 'Mr Dark,' he said. 'Why is your pocket vibrating?'

If it's possible for a person to look more busted than Felonious Dark did right then, I haven't seen it.

'Ah, it's not my pocket,' Felonious Dark said quickly, composing himself. 'I swallowed a fly. It must be buzzing around in my stomach.'

If it's possible for three children to look less convinced by a response than Kipp, Tobias and Cymphany did right then, I haven't seen that either. But, then again, there are lots of things I haven't seen.

But Kipp, Tobias and Cymphany didn't have time to quiz Felonious Dark about the super-fly that seemed to be able to survive in his stomach, even with all the stomach acid swishing about in there. They had a spooky house to visit.

8

A Ghost Train and a Top Hat

I am not a huge fan of ghost-train rides at fairgrounds for a number of reasons.

Reason number one: most of the time these trains do not actually take you anywhere. They go around in a loop, ending with you back where you began. Honestly, if the inventor of the train—who I'm sure was dedicated to the transportation of people from one location to another—found out their invention was being used to take people back to where they'd started, they would probably die of shock, if they weren't already dead, which I guess they are, because trains have been around for a long time.

Reason number two: why would ghosts need to catch a train in the first place? They are see-through and they can swish through walls and so on—and I'm sure I've never seen a ghost in line for a train ticket to go to the coast for the weekend. The 'ghosts' on the ghost train aren't even on the train, are they? They are actually around the train and they're just people in bad costumes, jumping out from behind gravestones, which are really just painted lumps of foam. So the correct title for the train should be ordinary-people train that takes you nowhere, with unconvincing ghosts and spooky sounds along the way.

And reason number three: they give me the heebie jeebies.

Anyway, where was I? Oh, that's right. Kipp, Tobias, Cymphany and a still-vibrating Felonious Dark had hurried down from the top of the hill along various Digmont Drives and they now stood in front of the House of Spooks.

'It looks like something out of the ghost-train ride they have at the Huggabie Falls Annual Fair,' Kipp said.

The black, towering, wonky house had scarecrows of ghosts and skeletons and werewolves in the overgrown front yard. Spooky screams were being blasted from speakers attached to the house. And there were signs that read 'Enter If You Dare' and 'Your Doom Awaits Inside' and 'Deliveries Around the Back, Please'.

When Kipp mentioned that the house reminded him of one of those appalling ghost-train rides, Felonious Dark's face brightened. 'Oh, I love ghost-train rides,' he said, which just goes to show you Felonious Dark was still a suspiciously strange individual, despite the fact that he claimed to be reformed.

Felonious Dark and Kipp, Tobias and Cymphany entered the House of Spooks through the rickety front door, which made a screaming noise when it opened. They pushed through spiderwebs into a tiny foyer, where a man wearing a top hat and a lab coat stood at a podium in front of a curtain door, which appeared to lead deeper into the house.

The man held his arms out wide. 'Welcome,' he boomed, 'to the House of Spooks, where your scariest and most'—he paused and pulled a scrap of paper from his pocket and glanced at it—'honourific nightmares will come true. Enter if you dare.'

Cymphany held up her favourite correcting finger, which was the one next to her thumb on her left hand. 'Ah, I think you mean *horrific* nightmares,' she said.

The man glanced at his bit of paper again and smiled thinly at her. 'Well, aren't you a smart little cookie? *Horrific* nightmares, yes,' he said. 'I am the proprietor of the House of Spooks. Rides on the ghost train are five dollars. And there are no free tickets under any circumstances.'

❖

Sorry to interrupt, but I just want to ask any readers out there who are keen correctors like Cymphany to please not write in to tell me the correct anatomical name for the finger next to the thumb. I think it might be called the index finger, but I didn't want to write that just in case I was wrong, and I didn't want to waste time rushing off to get a medical encyclopedia to look it up when Cymphany, Tobias and Kipp were just about to find out what has been going on in Huggabie Falls to cause all the unbelievably scary things that have been happening. Just saying it is the finger next to the thumb should be enough, as we all know which finger I'm talking about. But I can just see the letters now:

Dear Mr Cece,
I was really enjoying your book, *The Unbelievably Scary Thing that Happened in Huggabie Falls*, which was much better than I expected— it is an incredible, tantalising and captivating sequel, perhaps

even better than book one, and
obviously written by a dashing
and heroic author. But then I
got up to the bit about Cymphany
holding up her index finger and
I had to throw my book across the
room in disgust. How can you not
know the most basic names for
parts of the human body!
You numbskull.

Signed,
Smug Know-It-All

I've got a few things to say about anyone who might write a letter like this:

How dare you call me a numbskull!

Stop wasting my, and everyone else's, time, with your rant about what fingers are called. No one cares, and everyone wants to just find out what is going to happen to Kipp, Tobias and Cymphany, and Felonious Dark, in the House of Spooks, and they don't want to sit about and wait while you carry on about fingers.

But I almost forgive you already, because of the lovely thing you wrote about my sequel being captivating and about me being dashing and heroic. I must confess to being both of those things. Your kind words have just brightened up my whole day. So I do forgive you. In fact, I'm thinking about buying you a present.

Now, where was I? Oh, that's right. Kipp, Tobias and Cymphany had just entered the House of Spooks with Felonious Dark, and Cymphany had just corrected the man in the top hat and lab coat, by holding up her index finger, which I know is the correct name for it now, because after all that I went and looked it up in a medical encyclopedia.

Kipp raised his hand, as if he was at school and wanted to ask a question, which he wasn't but it did get the man's attention. 'Excuse me, but why are you wearing a lab coat?' he said. 'Are you a scientist?'

Tobias shuddered. 'We've had run-ins with scientists before, and you can probably tell from my shudder that they weren't good run-ins.'

The top-hatted man laughed. 'No, of course I'm not a scientist. Scientists aren't the only people who wear lab coats, you know.'

Cymphany scrunched up her brow. 'Umm... they sort of are.'

And I agree with Cymphany, so we are going to refer to this man as the top-hatted scientist from now on.

The top-hatted scientist shooed away Cymphany's comments. 'That's ridiculous. Scientists wear lab coats, yes, but so do lab-coat models, and House of Spooks proprietors, which is what I am.' The top-hatted scientist stopped when he looked at Felonious Dark. 'Wait a minute, do I know you from somewhere?'

Kipp, Tobias and Cymphany looked at Felonious Dark, as if to say, Mr Dark, is there something you haven't been telling us? We trusted you and now we think that might not have been a very smart thing to do.

Felonious Dark frowned. 'No, I don't think

so,' he said. 'I've never even been to somewhere.'

The top-hatted scientist looked puzzled for a moment, but then he smiled. 'My mistake,' he said. 'There's probably lots of people in this town who are tall and thin and evil-looking.'

'No there aren't,' said Kipp, holding up an index finger, as he'd obviously learnt about correcting people from Cymphany.

'Oh, look,' said the top-hatted scientist, producing four printed cards from behind the podium. 'You have won four free tickets for the House of Spooks ghost train. Congratulations. In you go.' And he swept the curtain aside to reveal a dimly lit passage.

'Wait a minute,' said Cymphany. 'You said no free tickets under any circumstances.'

The top-hatted scientist glared at her. 'That doesn't sound like something I'd say. In you go.' And he ushered them through the curtain doorway and swished it shut behind them. Kipp, Tobias and Cymphany heard the sound of a bolt sliding across somewhere on the other side of the curtain.

'Wait a minute?' Felonious Dark said, pushing the curtain. It didn't budge. 'How does a curtain lock, anyway? And fancy that man saying I looked evil. Can't he see I'm reformed?'

Cymphany smiled. 'Well, you are wearing a T-shirt with 'Don't Trust Me, I'm Evil' on it.'

Felonious Dark crossed his arms and harrumphed with annoyance. 'Well, I'm not going to throw out all my T-shirts just because I'm reformed, am I?'

But Kipp, Tobias and Cymphany didn't answer him. They had already begun exploring the dingy hallway. At the end they found a mini train track, with four inter-linked carts on it: one, conveniently, for each of them.

On the wall was a sign that read:

THE HOUSE OF SPOOKS

Creepy, spooky, unbelievably **SCARY** ghost-train ride begins <u>here</u>.

WARNING: Keep all limbs inside the cart while it is moving, and while it is stopped, and…well just keep your limbs inside the cart at all times.

Cymphany, Tobias and Kipp climbed into the first three carts, which left Felonious Dark to climb into the back cart, which was so small that he had to bend his legs so tight that his knees were above his head.

'Comfy back there, Mr Dark?' Tobias asked.

'Pardon?' Felonious Dark yelled. 'I can't hear anything. My thighs are covering my ears.'

The small train jerked and screeched and started clanking along the rusty tracks. It went through doorways, creaking along, crawling slowly from room to room through the House of Spooks.

'It's like an indoor rollercoaster,' Kipp said, looking around the spooky, dim rooms as they inched through each one.

'The most boring rollercoaster ever,' Cymphany yawned, 'without any up and down fun bits.'

The rooms were old and dusty, full of rather unconvincing statues of ghouls and creatures, with crackly screams and evil cackles coming

from speakers in each room. Bats and spiders on bouncing strings dropped down in front of the train every now and then, and one of these hit Cymphany on her head, which she found irritating, and not at all scary, despite the warning signs that read:

> **WARNING**
> Even more SCARINESS ahead.
> Apologies in advance for causing
> uncontrollable screaming.

'I'm not sure this is the place we're after,' Kipp said after about five boring rooms, not even flinching when a mop with teeth loomed up beside him. It took him a few moments to realise it was supposed to be a werewolf. 'It's hard to believe any of the unbelievably scary stuff happening in Huggabie Falls came from here.'

And just then Tobias jumped out of his cart, ignoring another red warning sign, which read:

WARNING

Riders should not leave the ride for any reasons whatsoever. No I mean it, no one should put so much as one toe out of their cart for **ANY** reason. I'm not mucking around, no reason. Even if you find a deadly python in your cart, you still shouldn't get out. Please just calmly call for an attendant, who will come and remove the python from your cart at their earliest convenience, usually within ten to fifteen minutes. So, I repeat, do not leave your cart during the ride. And anyway you wouldn't find a python in your cart in the first place, because only one rider is allowed in each cart at a time.

As Tobias ducked under a flying pillowcase with eye holes cut in it, which may or may not have been meant to resemble a ghost, Cymphany, who most of the time was quite a fan of rules, said, 'Ah, Tobias. I don't think you're supposed to leave the ride, even if there's a python in your cart. I mean, what part of that sign over there are you not getting?'

But Tobias had already disappeared into a dark doorway behind a painted-foam gravestone.

Kipp looked at Cymphany. She glared back at him and said, 'Don't even think about following him.'

So Kipp took his friend's advice, and didn't think about it, he just did it. He jumped out of his slow-moving cart and followed Tobias.

'Where is everyone going,' Felonious Dark yelled way too loud in the small echoey room—his legs were still blocking his ears.

Cymphany sat in her cart for a few seconds, looking at the doorway Kipp and Tobias had disappeared into. Then she sighed. 'Fiddlesticks,' she said, and she got out of her cart and followed her friends.

Felonious Dark watched her go, and he jerked and wriggled, trying to get at least one leg out of the cart. 'Ah, kids,' he said. 'I'll meet you at the other end. I think I'm stuck. Also, didn't any of you see the sign?'

9

The (Not So) Top-Secret Lab

Kipp and Cymphany followed Tobias through the doorway, to find it led down a hallway with a door at the end that had a big red warning sign on it.

Cymphany shook her head. 'Whoever runs this place is obsessed with warning signs. I just passed one that read: "Warning, warning sign ahead".'

Tobias and Kipp agreed the warning signage in the House of Spooks was a tad overdone.

They all read this latest warning sign:

> **WARNING**
> Top-Secret Lab.
> Do Not Enter.
>
> P.S. How did you get here?
> No one is supposed to
> leave their cart mid-ride.
> Didn't you see the sign?

'Whoever designed this sign isn't very smart,' Cymphany said. 'I mean, the lab isn't very top secret if there's a sign on the door that says "Top Secret", is it? It would be better if the sign said "Broom Cupboard".'

'Or totally-not-top-secret lab,' Tobias said.

Kipp ignored him. 'Shall we go in?' he said.

Tobias nodded enthusiastically. 'Do ostriches fly?'

Cymphany frowned at him and held up her now-famous correcting index finger. 'Actually, Tobias, ostriches can't fly.'

Tobias stopped. 'Oh, well in that case let's

just pretend I asked a question to which the answer is "yes".'

Cymphany put her hands on her hips. 'You know it would have been a lot quicker if you'd just said yes.'

'Let's just go in,' Tobias said. 'We're wasting time standing here talking about whether it would have been quicker if I hadn't brought ostriches into the conversation, and'—he paused and looked around—'hey, where's Kipp?'

The door was open, and Kipp was gone.

Cymphany and Tobias looked at each other.

Cymphany gulped. Tobias gulped. And without another word they both stepped through the doorway and into another hallway, where they found Kipp standing in front of a door. This hallway was even darker than the last one. But they could just make out another red warning sign on the wall.

The sign read:

Now, I must assure you at this point that I will
not continue to describe every warning sign that
Kipp, Tobias and Cymphany see as they venture
further towards the secret lab. Needless to say,
there are a lot of warning signs in the House of
Spooks, and Kipp, Tobias and Cymphany are
still going to see lots more of them, and they
will completely ignore every single one of them.
If I told you what all the warning signs said, it
would fill this whole book, and it would have
to be renamed *Warning: Warning Signs Galore*.
So I'll just make that the last warning sign I
write out.

It occurs to me that whoever is in charge of

the House of Spooks should have spent less time putting red warning signs up everywhere and more time making sure the door to the secret lab was actually locked.

Right-o, now that we've got that sorted, where was I? Ah yes, that's right. Kipp, Tobias and Cymphany had ignored the warning signs, all seven hundred and ninety-eight of them, and had ventured down several hallways and discovered the secret lab and opened the unlocked door and stepped inside.

The secret lab was a big circular room with a domed ceiling and a walkway that ran high around it. Cymphany found some steps, and Kipp and Tobias followed her up to the walkway.

They all peered down to see a circular platform in the middle of the room, which had what looked like a ring of hairdryers on stands around it.

'Well,' Kipp whispered. 'Either that's a machine that dries hair in under four seconds, or something weird is going on down there.'

Beside the platform was a chair, with a tied-up man sitting in it. He wore a helmet with cables attached to it, and he was facing a large flatscreen television.

The top-hatted scientist, whom Kipp, Tobias and Cymphany had met in the foyer of the House of Spooks earlier, stood at a control panel with lots of flashing lights on it, on the other side of the hairdryer things.

'Who is that tied-up man?' Cymphany asked. 'Is it...'

'Yes, it is. It's Conrad Creeps,' Tobias said, alarmed.

Conrad Creeps was a well-known Huggabie Falls local. His weirdness was that he was scared of everything—absolutely everything. From pencils to pelicans, if it existed Conrad was scared of it. Conrad was even scared of not being scared of anything, so it was just as well he was scared of everything, but, then again, he was also scared of everything. As you can

imagine Conrad Creeps had a lot of trouble getting anything done. He once tried to go for a walk but found it quite impossible because he was scared of streets, people, fences, hedges, air, sunlight and, worst of all, he was scared of walking. So it was very unusual to see Conrad outside his house. But he was also scared of staying at home. As you can see, talking about Conrad Creeps for too long can easily give you a headache, and I don't want to give you a headache (which, by the way, is another thing Conrad is scared of), so I'll stop talking about him now.

Kipp, Tobias and Cymphany watched poor, tied-up Conrad Creeps and worried he might be scared. Actually there was no *might* about it, Conrad was always scared, but in this particular case he seemed to have a very good reason to be scared.

'We should call the police,' Cymphany whispered. 'If only we had a mobile phone.'

Kipp paused for a second, watching Conrad,

and shook his head. 'Let's hope the ghost-train ride has finished, and Mr Dark has worked out something fishy is going on round here and has called for help.'

Little did they know the ghost-train ride had finished some time ago, but Felonious Dark was still stuck in his cart and, because his legs were squashed close to his ears, he couldn't reach into his pocket for his phone. But he was currently screaming for help, even though a warning sign beside him read:

WARNING
No screaming.

Tobias nodded. 'If I know Mr Dark, the police will be here any moment,' he said. Which just goes to show Tobias didn't know Felonious Dark at all.

Far below, a squirming Conrad Creeps was talking to the top-hatted scientist.

'Please let me go. I'm scared of being tied up. Come to think of it, I'm scared of everything in this room, including that pencil over there, and scientists in top hats, and *especially* beeping helmets.'

The top-hatted scientist furrowed his brow—furrowing brows was another thing Conrad was completely petrified of. 'Why does everyone keep assuming I'm a scientist just because I wear a lab coat? And anyway, there's no reason to be scared—all we're going to do is show you a few hundred more scary things and make a few hundred more scare balls—one for every person in town. That doesn't sound too scary does it?'

Conrad's eyes popped open. 'That sounds like the scariest thing ever.'

'Scare ball?' Cymphany whispered to Kipp and Tobias. 'What is a scare ball?'

Tobias shrugged. 'Do you think it has something to do with the unbelievably scary things that are happening?'

'I think'—Kipp pointed to the platform below—'we're about to find out.'

'Well, okay then,' the top-hatted scientist said to Conrad Creeps. 'We don't want to keep you here against your will so you're free to go. I'll get my assistant to release you. Unless...' The top-hatted scientist smirked. 'You're afraid of being let go.'

Conrad's face twisted in fear. 'Fine,' he said. 'I can't work out which thing I'm most scared of, but change is something particularly scary, so let's keep doing this.'

The top-hatted scientist laughed. 'Very well. Assistant, would you please turn on the Scare-a-Build 1000.'

At that moment a door opened at the side of the secret lab and a tall thin man in a striped suit walked in smiling and carrying a remote control. Conrad gasped. He was scared of smiling—it gave him shivers up his spine. But the smiling was a secondary concern—it was the remote control that was the most terrifying.

Remote controls had buttons, and buttons were the *worst*!

When Kipp, Tobias and Cymphany saw who the man was they all gasped too, and then quickly clamped their hands over their mouths so they wouldn't be heard.

'That's the last person I expected to see,' Kipp whispered.

The man with the remote control was, as you might have guessed, Felonious Dark.

10

Scare Balls

I've always been annoyed by the expression 'the last person you expected to see'. Now, I don't want to accuse Kipp of not telling the truth, but, when you think about it, Felonious Dark was in no way the last person he would have expected to see. The last person he would have expected to see would have probably been someone like Genghis Khan, because: a) he's a famous ruler of the Mongolian Empire, and rulers of Mongolian Empires rarely ever visited

Huggabie Falls in the winter, and b) he's been dead for almost eight hundred years. And even Genghis Khan wouldn't have been the last person Kipp would have expected to see—say if Julius Caesar, or Tutankhamun, all wrapped up in mummy bandages, walked in, then I think everyone would have been really surprised. But Felonious Dark was probably not even in the top one hundred people Kipp least expected to see. Even so, considering the fact that Felonious Dark was supposed to be on the ghost-train ride, and he'd looked like he didn't even know the top-hatted scientist when he'd met him earlier, Kipp was quite surprised to see him.

'It's Mr Dark,' Tobias said, which earned him yes-thank-you-we-can-see-that looks from Kipp and Cymphany.

'What's he doing here?' Kipp asked.

'I think we're about to find out,' Cymphany replied.

As Felonious Dark turned on the flatscreen television—which was attached to the big platform and the hairdryer things, which, as the top-hatted scientist had pointed out, was a Scare-a-Build 1000—he told Conrad Creeps to relax. But relaxing terrified Conrad, so he shut his eyes. But then Felonious Dark reminded him that he was also scared of shutting his eyes. So Conrad opened them again.

Kipp, Tobias and Cymphany couldn't see what Conrad Creeps could see on the screen, but they could see his horrified face. 'Turn it off! Turn it off!' Conrad screamed. 'It's horrible. It's terrifying. Please. Turn it off!'

Cymphany gulped. 'Wow, they must be showing Conrad something really scary,' she said.

'Yes,' said Kipp. 'It could be anything.'

The helmet Conrad was wearing started to blink and flash and make a humming noise. The wires attached to the helmet began to hum too, and jiggle, and Kipp, Tobias and Cymphany saw now that these wires were attached to the platform with the hairdryer things around the edge of it.

Suddenly, laser beams shot out of the hairdryer things, and these laser beams collided above the centre of the platform, sending sparks into the air. The hairdryer things swished left and right, sending the laser beams criss-crossing, until they began to form a mesh pattern, and soon the mesh pattern began to form a shape.

'Wow,' Cymphany said. 'That's amazing technology.'

'Is it?' said Tobias. 'I have no idea what's going on.'

'If I had to guess,' Cymphany said, sounding like a person who was often right when she guessed, 'I'd say that we're looking at a hard-light-hologram-generation machine. Sort of like a 3D printer, but it forms things out of hard laser light.'

Kipp frowned. 'That can't be possible. How can a thing be made out of laser light?'

'Look. The thing is almost finished,' Tobias said, pointing. And Kipp and Cymphany looked. In the middle of the platform the hairdryer things were putting the final touches on a thing, which was now standing fully formed and fully coloured, and the thing was...

Now it was Cymphany's turn to frown. 'A pigeon?' she said.

The lasers stopped. And the thing that had formed—the pigeon—started moving. Its claws made little clacks on the metal platform as it bobbed about and cooed, seemingly searching for birdseed on the flat metal surface.

Tobias gawked at the pigeon. 'It's alive,' he said. 'But how can it be alive? It's made of laser light.'

Cymphany shook her head. 'It's not alive. It's a computer generation of a pigeon made of hard laser light. It's quite impressive when you think about it.'

Felonious Dark did not look impressed. He spun the screen towards the top-hatted scientist, and Kipp, Tobias and Cymphany could now see what was on it. It was a picture of a glob of pigeon poo in someone's hair.

'It didn't work,' Felonious Dark said. 'I thought Conrad Creeps was supposed to imagine the most horrifying version of whatever we put on the screen.'

But just as he said that the pigeon took off and started circling above Conrad Creeps, and Conrad Creeps wailed, because he knew what was coming—after all, he was the one who had imagined it.

What happened next truly was terrifying. The pigeon began to poo. But this was no ordinary pigeon, and this was no ordinary pigeon poo. It was as if the pigeon had a cannon in its behind and it

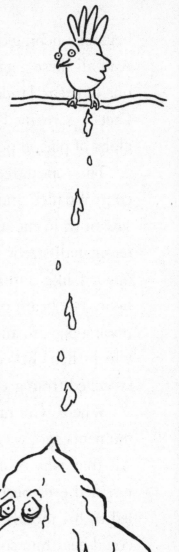

began launching colossal mounds of pigeon poo. And all these gigantic pigeon poos, every single one of them, landed on Conrad Creeps. Conrad Creeps screamed with horror as the gigantic globs of pigeon poo pelted down relentlessly.

The top-hatted scientist hit a button on his control panel, and Kipp, Tobias and Cymphany saw now, in the middle of the platform, a small tennis-ball-sized metal ball that clicked and opened like a flower, and emitted a beam of light. The beam of light hooked onto the flying, pooing pigeon, and sucked the bird into the ball, which then clicked shut, and a light on the ball switched from green to red.

Where Conrad Creeps had been sitting moments ago, was now just a pile of pigeon poo. All that was visible of poor Conrad were his terrified eyes peering out and a small hole that led to his mouth. Kipp, Tobias and Cymphany could hear him sobbing.

The top-hatted scientist stepped up onto the platform and picked up the small metal ball, which now contained a super-pooing pigeon.

Four women in lab coats, who were presumably scientist henchwomen, wheeled a giant wooden crate into the room, which was full of hundreds of metal balls, all seemingly identical to the one the top-hatted scientist was holding.

The top-hatted scientist tossed the ball he was holding into the air, and just before it hit the lab floor, eight legs sprang from it. It landed like a spider and scuttled across the floor, its eight little feet making hundreds of tiny *click-clack* noises. Then it launched itself back into the air, landed in the crate and its legs retracted.

Felonious Dark cracked up laughing, not at the spider ball, but at the mound of pigeon poo that contained Conrad Creeps. 'Oh that was fantastic. I tell you, if I was scared of a pigeon pooing on my shirt, that would *definitely* be enough to drive me out of town. I'm mean I'm not scared of a pigeon pooing on my shirt, and I still think that would be enough to drive me out of town!'

'I don't get it,' Tobias said, sharing a confused look with Kipp and Cymphany. 'What does all this mean? Apart from Conrad Creeps, who else is scared of pigeons pooing on them?'

'Miss Gilly Ganderfence,' Kipp said. 'She lives down the road from me, on Digmont Drive. She's petrified of pigeons pooing on her. Every time she leaves the house she carries an umbrella, and even then, if she sees a pigeon she runs back to her house screaming.'

Tobias chuckled. 'She'd better hope that she never runs into that super-pooing pigeon. No umbrella is going to stop that poo.'

Cymphany glared at Tobias.

Tobias gave her a blank look back. 'What?' he said.

'Don't you get it, Tobias?' Cymphany said. 'Froggin Fillibuster was petrified of spiders, and he found a two-metre-tall spider in his kitchen. Yorrick Yugel was scared of sharks, and, inexplicably, one ended up in the vault of his bank. And the Dinosaur Fearers Anonymous group...'

'A Tyrannosaurus Rex,' Kipp said slowly. He and Cymphany nodded at each other.

Tobias looked back and forth between them. 'Why do I feel like I'm the only one who has no idea what's going on here?' he said.

'Those metal balls,' Cymphany explained, '*obviously* contain hard-light holograms. Those holograms are *obviously* the most terrifying versions of people's fears, which only Conrad Creeps could dream up, and I'm pretty sure they are being made to target specific people and their specific fears. Somehow the top-hatted scientist is going to make sure that his latest scare ball thingy gets to Gilly Ganderfence, and when it opens and projects that pigeon again, it's going to be Gilly's worst nightmare come true.'

'But why?' asked Kipp. 'Why would anyone want to do this?'

At this point, the top-hatted scientist clicked his fingers and the four scientist henchwomen fetched shovels and began shovelling the pigeon poo away. Eventually, they revealed a shivering, poo-covered Conrad underneath.

'Please, no more,' Conrad blubbered. 'I can't take any more.'

'Well, lucky for you, Conrad,' said Felonious Dark as he checked a clipboard. 'That was the last one for today.'

'Actually'—the top-hatted scientist raised an interrupting finger (an index finger again, for all you finger buffs out there)— 'I think we'll do one more.'

Conrad Creeps wailed.

Felonious Dark frowned. 'Are you sure?' He

flipped a page on his clipboard. 'We've done two hundred and thirty-seven today already.'

'It's a special one,' said the top-hatted scientist, with an evil grin.

Felonious Dark shrugged. 'Whatever. You're the boss.' And he turned the flatscreen back towards Conrad and clicked the remote control to bring up a new image.

'Oh, no.' Conrad's lip trembled. 'Not that,' he yelped. 'Anything but that.'

Kipp, Tobias and Cymphany couldn't see the screen, but Cymphany shook her head. 'This image must be very scary. Poor Conrad.'

The helmet atop Conrad's head flashed and hummed, and the laser-shooting hairdryer things flared into action again. The pigeon was only a small thing, but this thing was even smaller. It took only a few seconds for it to form. It was approximately egg-sized, with tiny arms and legs, and it was green.

Kipp squinted at the thing. 'It's a Brussels sprout. A Brussels sprout with teeny arms and legs, and…is that a miniature kilt it's wearing?

'It's so cute,' said Cymphany.

Felonious Dark stared at the tiny kilted Brussels sprout in shock, but the top-hatted scientist smiled his evil smile at it. 'Hello,' he said.

And to everyone's amazement the Brussels sprout spoke back. 'Hello,' he said. 'I'm here to do a wee bit of poundin'. So get oot of ma way.'

Cymphany's mouth dropped open. 'Is that Brussels sprout speaking in a very bad Scottish accent?'

Kipp raised his eyebrows. 'Who in their right mind is scared of a Brussels sprout that speaks with a very bad Scottish accent?'

It seems Felonious Dark had the same thought, because he said, 'Who in their right mind is scared of a Brussels sprout that speaks with a very bad Scottish accent?'

'Aye, who is it? The numpty,' the Brussels sprout said.

The top-hatted scientist laughed. 'It's for

our little intruder, hiding in the dome with his friends.'

Kipp and Cymphany locked eyes, confused, and then they turned and looked at Tobias. His face was even whiter than usual, which was really saying something because Tobias's face was naturally pearly white. And now he was frozen in an expression of absolute terror.

Below them, the top-hatted scientist said, 'This scare-ball creature is for Tobias Treachery.'

If You Scare Easily Skip this Chapter

'Run first and ask questions later', is one of my all-time favourite expressions, along with 'between a rock and a hard place', and 'never tickle a buffalo while it is watching daytime television'. It is generally a good idea to run first and ask questions later, unless you are competing in the annual Huggabie Falls Marathon Quiz. The word *marathon* is sometimes used to refer to something that lasts a really long time, and while the annual Huggabie Falls Marathon

Quiz is quite lengthy, it is also a quiz held at the same time as its participants run a forty-two-kilometre marathon. So the participants of this event do not run first and ask questions later, they run and ask (or rather answer) questions at the same time.

Now Kipp, like me, was a big fan of the expression 'run first and ask questions later', so when the top-hatted scientist had just used the big laser thing-creating machine to create a fearful object—and had revealed that this object was for Tobias Treachery, and had pointed at Kipp, Tobias and Cymphany, indicating he knew they were there—Kipp's first instinct was to run. But he also wanted to ask a rather big question, which was: who in their right mind is scared of a Brussels sprout that speaks with a very bad Scottish accent?

'Yes, that's right,' the top-hatted scientist called out. 'We've known you children were there the whole time. We have a secret surveillance camera hidden in the dot above every i in every warning sign in this place. Why do you think there are so many warning signs?'

'Oh.' Cymphany nodded. 'That makes sense. That's actually quite a clever idea.'

'Cymphany!' Kipp said, as if the expression 'run first and ask questions later', should be changed to, 'run first and congratulate the top-hatted scientist on a good place to hide secret surveillance cameras later'. But that second version of the expression probably wouldn't work very well, as it's quite specific, although if that expression did exist I personally could have used it three times this week alone.

As Kipp, Tobias and Cymphany ran back along the walkway towards the stairs, they noticed a door with a sign above it that read 'Escape Exit' and a warning sign beside it that read:

```
WARNING
Door opens inwards.
```

It took Tobias quite a few seconds to open the door, because he tried to push it instead of pulling it, and I'd like to say there is an important lesson here about reading warning signs, even ones with hidden surveillance cameras in them.

As they ran down a stairwell, which must have been an escape exit, Kipp asked, 'Tobias, are you really scared of Brussels sprouts with very bad Scottish accents?' Kipp had obviously decided to run and ask questions at the same time, even though this wasn't the annual Huggabie Falls Marathon Quiz.

And Cymphany added to Kipp's question by saying, 'I thought you loved Brussels sprouts, Tobias.'

'I used to,' Tobias said, bounding down the steps. 'I used to eat them all the time. For just about every meal. I loved them with chicken salt and tomato sauce, especially in sandwiches and on pizzas.'

They continued tearing down the steps at top speed. Above them they heard the door to the escape exit bang open. 'But then,' Tobias continued, 'I read a book called, *Do Vegetables Have Feelings?* And I started to wonder, do vegetables have feelings? And if they do, then Brussels sprouts are going to be so annoyed that I have eaten thousands of them. Then I started having terrible nightmares about an evil Scottish Brussels sprout coming to get revenge for all the members of his Brussels sprout family I've consumed. It's my biggest fear, actually.'

'But why is it a Scottish Brussels sprout,' Cymphany said, breathlessly. 'And why does it talk with such a terrible accent. That's not how Scottish people really talk, you know.'

Tobias glared at Cymphany. 'I don't know. I didn't get to write a script for my nightmares, did I? Nightmares just happen. I think the first time I had the nightmare I was watching a movie that day, with an actor in it, who had a terrible fake Scottish accent, his name was Mel—'

Cymphany interrupted him. 'Better not say the actor's full name, Tobias, just in case someday someone writes a book about our adventures. We don't want the actor with the terrible fake Scottish accent to get upset and come after us for revenge.'

Now it was Kipp's turn to glare at Cymphany. 'Cymphany, why would somebody write a book about our adventures one day? And even if they did, this is our second adventure, so this book would be a sequel, and no one is silly enough to write one of those. Secondly, I hardly think that is our major worry right now.'

As Kipp, Tobias and Cymphany continued hurtling down the steps three at a time, they could hear tiny footsteps on the steps above them, and a squeaky, but gruff, voice saying, 'Oi. Where d'ye think ye can run ta? I'm a comin' fer ye.'

I should point out, at this point, in case you are worried, that vegetables most certainly do not have feelings. And you can feel free to keep eating vegetables—in fact you should eat them, as they are quite healthy—without fear of attack from any of their vegetable cousins.

'Okay,' Cymphany said, upon hearing Tobias's story about why he was scared of Brussels sprouts with very bad Scottish accents, 'that makes sense.' Of course, she was lying about it making sense, but she was under a lot of pressure, and running for her life, so she was happy to have just about any explanation at this point.

A few steps later Kipp, Tobias and Cymphany reached a door at the bottom of the escape exit.

They burst out the door, to be confronted by hundreds of identical versions of their shocked faces staring back at them.

'Oh, no,' said Cymphany, 'there are mirrors everywhere. We must have run full pelt into the storage yard for the Huggabie Falls Mirror Emporium.'

Kipp, Tobias and Cymphany ran across the yard, weaving between mirrors of all different shapes and sizes. Everywhere they turned they saw reflections of themselves looking back, and reflections of those reflections in mirrors all around them, which gave the weird sense of hundreds of them all running in different directions. It was like trying to escape through a confusing giant crowd of yourself.

Behind them somewhere, Kipp, Tobias and Cymphany heard the door to the House of Spooks escape exit open, and a small voice say 'Och, that's a good-lookin fellow.' The Scottish Brussels sprout had obviously seen his own reflection.

Kipp, Tobias and Cymphany kept running. They finally stumbled into an open area free of mirrors, but it was surrounded by a high fence. They ran towards the fence, looking for a way over it. But there were no rungs to climb, or any doors or gaps to squeeze through.

'We have to go back,' said Kipp.

'Ye cannae go back,' a voice said. 'I'm here fur ye.'

They spun around, backs to the fence, to

see one hundred Brussels sprouts with very bad Scottish accents standing in a row.

'Time ta introduce ye ta all ma pals,' the Brussels sprout with the very bad Scottish accent in the middle of the row said, while all the other Brussels sprouts moved their lips at the same time.

'Oh, no,' Tobias said as he cowered. 'This is all my nightmares come true. And now there's hundreds of them. We're done for.'

But Kipp stopped and stood up. 'Wait a minute. There are not hundreds of them. There's just

one Brussels sprout reflected hundreds of times. And he's tiny.'

Cymphany smiled and nodded. 'I know, right. Just because Tobias is scared of him, doesn't mean we have to be too. What possible damage could one little Brussels sprout do?'

Kipp and Cymphany both laughed at the absurdity of the situation. But then Tobias said, 'Ah, guys.'

They looked at him.

Tobias gulped. 'I forgot to mention that in my nightmares the Brussels sprout has super-human strength, and he is always trying to crush me with a grand piano.'

A hint of concern flashed across Cymphany's face, but she was still smiling. 'Tobias, the hard-light-hologram generator didn't create a grand piano.'

'I think it did,' Tobias said, trembling with fear.

'No, we were there. It definitely didn't,' Kipp said.

Tobias tried to speak but he was shaking

so much even he couldn't understand what he was saying, so he pointed. Cymphany and Kipp turned just in time to see a grand piano flying through the air towards them.

Cymphany, Kipp and Tobias dived out of the way, and the grand piano smashed into the ground, splintering into thousands of pieces. Bits of wood and piano keys rained down all around Kipp, Cymphany and Tobias as they scrambled out of the debris.

'Honestly, Tobias,' Cymphany said, as a piano key bounced off her head, with a pitch-perfect middle C. 'Why can't you just have normal nightmares?'

'I'm sorry,' Tobias yelped, as keys pounded the ground all around him in an amazing chance order to play the tune 'Happy Birthday'. If Kipp, Tobias and Cymphany hadn't been running for their lives, they could have stopped to admire this once in a gazillion lifetimes event, but Cymphany was too busy yelling at Tobias and Kipp to keep running.

Kipp, Tobias and Cymphany ran between some mirrors and around a corner, and then skidded to a stop in terror.

Standing in front of them were at least a hundred Felonious Darks.

The one hundred Felonious Darks smiled. 'Hello, children,' they all said. 'I managed to get off the ghost-train ride, but now I'm a bit lost in this yard of mirrors.'

Kipp, Tobias and Cymphany stared in shock at the one hundred Felonious Darks.

'It's only one Mr Dark,' Cymphany whispered to Kipp and Tobias, 'reflected a hundred times, like the Brussels sprout was.'

'Did you find anything?' the Felonious Dark in the middle said, and his hundred reflections moved their lips at exactly the same time. 'I think something fishy is going on in this place. I keep hearing whirring camera noises behind the warning signs, and a few minutes ago I heard a big crashing noise followed by somebody playing 'Happy Birthday' on a piano.'

'Mr Dark,' Cymphany said, stamping her foot. 'Don't lie to us. We know you've been helping the top-hatted scientist and torturing poor Conrad Creeps, and because of you we're being chased by a revenge-driven Brussels sprout with a very bad Scottish accent who's trying to flatten us with a grand piano.'

Felonious Dark raised an eyebrow, along with the other hundred Felonious Darks. 'Me, helping the top-hatted scientist? I don't think so. I'm pretty sure I would remember something like that. And Conrad Creeps? Isn't he the guy who's scared of everything? And did you say a Brussels sprout with a very bad Scottish accent is trying to flatten you with a grand piano?'

Just as Cymphany started to say, yes a Brussels sprout with a very bad Scottish accent is trying to flatten us with a grand piano, the giant mirror beside Felonious Dark shattered into a thousand pieces as a grand piano came flying through it. Felonious Dark ducked and the piano whizzed over his head, before crashing into the ground and bouncing away—smashing through mirrors like a grand-piano-shaped wrecking ball. It left a trail of shattered glass, which made a jagged path towards what appeared to be an exit doorway in the fence.

Felonious Dark turned to see where the grand piano had come from and his jaw dropped. The Brussels sprout smiled at him. 'Och aye, another noggin for flattenin. Looks like it's ma lucky day.'

Felonious Dark turned back to Kipp, Tobias and Cymphany. 'In reference to my questions before, you can ignore the third one. But I'm still quite curious about the first two things I asked about. I think we might have to revisit those queries at a future time—have you children ever heard of the expression: 'Run first and ask questions later'?

12

The Dark Family Business

Kipp, Tobias and Cymphany escaped from the Huggabie Falls Mirror Emporium via the exit door, and raced, ducking and weaving, through the streets of Huggabie Falls, which of course were all called Digmont Drive. Eventually they found a spot to hide in the now-abandoned—since Froggin Fillibuster had found a two-metre-tall spider in his kitchen—Huggabie Falls Sanctuary for People Fleeing from Witches and Other Dangerous Flying Creatures.

Felonious Dark had raced along behind them, and was now hiding with them. 'I can't see anything,' he whispered, as he shifted the curtains enough to form a hair-width crack and peeked out the front window of the sanctuary. 'I think he's gone.'

Since the sanctuary had been deserted, the tiny spider, who used to occupy a single high corner, had taken full advantage of the new situation and had built spiderwebs over every surface and object in the room.

Kipp, Tobias and Cymphany sat in a spiderweb-covered booth and glared at Felonious Dark. Felonious Dark saw them glaring and frowned. 'Look, I told you.' He threw up his hands. 'That wasn't me. I was stuck in the last cart on the ghost-train ride with my knees up above my head. I was only able to escape because I remembered I had a packet of butter in my pocket. I got it out with my teeth and used it to make myself slippery enough to slide out of the cart.'

Tobias nodded, smiling. 'Ah, that explains why I keep thinking of pancakes,' he said.

'And, like I keep saying,' Felonious Dark continued, 'the person you saw with the top-hatted scientist must have been my identical brother.'

'So you're a twin?' Kipp asked.

Felonious Dark shook his head. 'No. I'm not a twin.'

'Is anyone else confused?' Tobias asked. 'And hungry?'

Felonious Dark smiled, letting go of the edge of the curtain and sitting down in the spiderweb-covered booth across from Kipp, Tobias and Cymphany. 'I'm a triplet.'

'Identical triplets?' Cymphany frowned. 'Is that even possible?' she asked, quite annoyed that she didn't already know the answer to the question.

Felonious Dark sighed. 'It is possible. Of course it's possible. How else would I have two identical triplet brothers. I knew one of them was in town. He's been ringing me on my mobile phone all morning.'

Tobias slammed his hand down on the spiderweb-covered table. 'I knew it. I knew that vibrating noise was your mobile phone. I knew you hadn't eaten a particularly buzzy fly.'

'Oh, no,' Felonious Dark said. 'I had *also* been eating flies. But you're right, that vibrating noise was my identical triplet brother, ringing to tell me he'd come to town.' He took a deep breath. 'And it looks like he has gone into the family business.'

Kipp, Tobias and Cymphany gave Felonious

Dark matching blank looks. 'Which is?' Cymphany asked.

'Working for evil scientists, of course,' Felonious Dark said. 'I thought you would have worked that out by now. It's what my father did, my grandfather, my great-grandfather, my great-great-grandfather, my great-great-great-grandfather, my great-great-great-great—'

'Grandfather,' Cymphany finished his sentence. 'Yes, we get the picture.'

'Actually.' Felonious Dark held up a finger. 'I was going to say my great-great-great-great-great-grandfather, as my great-great-great-great-grandfather didn't work for an evil scientist. He was a peanut salesman.'

The blank looks Kipp, Tobias and Cymphany had given Felonious Dark before were barely blank looks at all compared to the blank looks they gave him now.

'Why did your great-great-great-great-grandfather sell peanuts?' Kipp asked.

Felonious Dark looked confused. 'I think he

liked peanuts,' he said.

'Look, we're getting sidetracked here,' said Cymphany crossly. 'What matters is why your brother is helping the top-hatted scientist scare everyone out of Huggabie Falls, and how we're going to stop them both.'

They thought in silence for a moment. Then Tobias said, 'When we were running away, I saw one of those spider balls.'

'I think the top-hatted scientist called them scare balls,' Kipp added.

Tobias nodded. 'Yes, that's them. I saw a scare ball scuttling along, on its spider legs, behind the Brussels sprout with the very bad Scottish accent. It was there the whole time.'

'Yes, I saw that scare ball too,' Cymphany said. 'And it makes sense. Hard-light holograms need a constant power-and-projection source.'

Tobias and Kipp and Felonious Dark stared at Cymphany.

'What?' Cymphany said defensively, looking from one of them to the other.

'How could you *possibly* know that?' Kipp asked.

Cymphany shrugged. 'I read it in a book.'

Tobias smirked and shook his head. 'Are there any books you *haven't* read, Cymph?'

Cymphany rolled her eyes. 'Don't be ridiculous, of course there are.' Although she had a little smirk on her face, too, because she was pretty sure she was down to fewer than ten left to be read before she'd read every single book ever written.

'But,' Tobias said, his smirk disappearing, 'there were hundreds of those spider scare balls in that crate. Hundreds of them.'

'Enough for one for everyone in town,' Kipp said, and he gulped.

'The whole spider design is fantastic,' Felonious Dark said. 'That way those fast little balls can skitter around town undetected, get near people and then project their greatest fears.' He chuckled. 'It's brilliant. That's exactly how I would do it.'

He saw Kipp, Tobias and Cymphany glaring at him and jumped. 'Errr...I mean, how I would do it, if I wasn't reformed. But, like I said, it wasn't me. It was my identical triplet brother.'

'So,' Kipp said slowly, turning his head away from Felonious Dark and back to Cymphany and Tobias. 'If we destroy the spider scare balls, we destroy the hard-light holograms, and if we destroy the hard-light holograms we destroy everyone's greatest fears?'

'It looks that way,' said Cymphany. 'But that won't do it entirely. Felonious Dark's identical triplet brother and the top-hatted scientist can just make more. To stop this for good we need to destroy the Scare-a-Build 1000 too. And we need to rescue poor Conrad Creeps. The unbelievably scary things seem to be generated from his particularly scaredy-cat mind.'

There was a noise outside, and everyone rushed to the curtain and peeked out, but it was just a truck from the Huggabie Falls Imaginary Creatures Zoo rumbling past.

As everyone sat back down again, Tobias asked, 'What's your identical triplet brother's name, Mr Dark?'

'His name,' Felonious Dark said, pausing for dramatic effect, 'is Felonious Dark Two.'

It must have been the day for blank looks, because Kipp, Tobias and Cymphany all looked so blank you could hardly see their eyes, mouths or noses.

It was quite some time before anyone spoke. Eventually, Kipp said, 'Felonious Dark too?'

'Wow,' Tobias said, 'it must be very confusing at family dinners if you both have the same name.'

Felonious Dark wasn't listening. He continued. 'Ever since we were children he thought he was better than me because his name is longer than mine.'

Cymphany blinked, as if to say, this is making no sense at all. 'But he has the same name as you,' she said.

Felonious Dark sat up straight. 'No, he does

not. I don't know where you got that idea. His name is Felonious Dark Two. T-W-O. He has three more letters in his name than I have in mine. Everyone knows that the longer your name is the better it is.'

'That's ridiculous,' Cymphany scoffed, while secretly being very pleased that the name Cymphany was two letters longer than the name Tobias and four letters longer than the name Kipp.

'It might be ridiculous,' Felonious Dark growled. 'But it has meant my brother has always been superior to me, and he's always let me know it. We haven't spoken in ten years... until he rang me today.'

Tobias laughed. 'I bet you're both pretty jealous of your third brother, then.'

Felonious Dark looked confused. 'Why?'

'Felonious Dark Three has more letters than both of you,' Tobias said, looking very proud of himself for working this out.

Felonious Dark chuckled. 'No way. He's got

it worse than anyone. You wouldn't believe what his name is.'

Kipp, Tobias and Cymphany leaned forward in anticipation. 'What is it?' Kipp asked.

Felonious Dark fixed his eyes on them. 'Al,' he said, very seriously. 'It's not even short for Alistair or Alvin, it's just Al. It was so humiliating for him that he packed his bags and left home when he was only four years old.'

Cymphany, Tobias and Kipp shared amused expressions. 'You know, Mr Dark,' Tobias said. 'I can't believe you and your family haven't always lived in Huggabie Falls. The Darks are certainly weird enough.'

For a moment everyone almost forgot that an hour ago they had been running from a Brussels sprout and dodging grand pianos, but then something scuttled across the countertop nearby.

'Scare ball!' Felonious Dark screamed, and everyone dived under the table. They cowered there, among the spiderwebs. After a few moments, Cymphany was brave enough to poke her head out.

When she saw what was scuttling across the countertop, she rolled her eyes, crawled out from under the booth table, and stood up. 'It's not a scare ball with spider legs. It's just a regular spider with spider legs.'

'A two-metre-tall spider?' Tobias squeaked.

Cymphany scoffed. 'More like a two-millimetre-tall spider.'

The tiny spider, who had been enjoying having this whole place to itself since Froggin had left, and was waiting patiently for these new occupants to clear off, was about to protest that it was actually two point seven millimetres tall, when Cymphany added, 'Anyway, it's an important reminder that we can't stay here for too much longer, doing nothing. We need to leave and get on with stopping the top-hatted scientist and Felonious Dark Two.'

Kipp, Tobias and Felonious Dark and, especially, the tiny spider all agreed.

As soon as they were reasonably confident there were no Brussels sprouts with very bad Scottish accents hiding outside, ready to jump out and throw grand pianos at them, Kipp, Tobias, Cymphany and Felonious Dark left the Huggabie Falls Sanctuary for People Fleeing from Witches and Other Dangerous Flying Creatures.

Felonious Dark headed straight for the police station to report the top-hatted scientist and Felonious Dark Two for kidnapping Conrad Creeps and for scaring Huggabie Falls residents with hard-light holograms projected from scare balls. 'And,' Felonious Dark said angrily, 'they need to make those carts at the House of Spooks quite a bit bigger so people don't get stuck in them. I've still got pins and needles in my legs.'

'That was all very bizarre,' Cymphany said, once Felonious Dark had disappeared down Digmont Drive, in the opposite direction from the way she and Kipp and Tobias were going.

Tobias nodded. 'I know. I can't believe Mr Dark eats flies. I mean, I've tried them—who hasn't? But it sounds like Mr Dark eats them often.'

Kipp and Cymphany stopped walking for five milliseconds and glanced at each other. Then they kept walking and looked straight ahead. It's interesting that in one five-millisecond shared look you can actually have an entire silent conversation. The conversation Kipp and Cymphany had in their five-millisecond look went something like this:

Are you thinking what I'm thinking?

Were you thinking, why would Tobias have tried eating flies?

Yes, that's exactly what I was thinking.

Do you want to ask him about it?

Ummm...not really.

Me neither, there are some questions you're better off not knowing the answer to, and I believe this is one of them.

I agree, shall we keep walking then.

Yes, let's.

So Cymphany and Kipp kept walking, not ignoring Tobias's bizarre comment about eating flies, but filing it away as something to bring up later.

'And what about Mr Dark being a triplet?' Tobias kept on chatting, unaware that a five-millisecond silent conversation about him eating flies had just taken place. 'I can't believe how much his brother looks like him.'

Cymphany and Kipp nodded in agreement. 'It's quite amazing,' Kipp said. 'They even wear the same suit.'

'Anyway,' Cymphany yawned, as they turned down Tobias's street, Digmont Drive. 'It's been a very long and tiring day. Let's all go home to bed, and by morning Mr Dark will have told the Huggabie Falls police officer about his identical triplet brother's dastardly dealings with the top-hatted scientist, and they'll have shut down that spooky House of Spooks and arrested the top-hatted scientist and Felonious Dark Two and there'll be no more hard-light holograms bursting out of spider scare balls and terrifying the people of Huggabie Falls.'

Kipp nodded. 'And everything will be back to normal.'

I'd like to just mention at this point that if that were to happen then I would be going back to my old job as a window cleaner of miniature model houses, because no one will want to read a book with an anti-climactic ending such as: And then Felonious Dark went to the police, the House of Spooks was shut down, and everything in Huggabie Falls went back to normal, which is to say back to weird.

But, lucky for me—because there just isn't enough work in cleaning the windows of miniature model houses because people don't care about their miniature model houses like they used to—that wasn't what happened next.

Here is what happened next.

At that moment Tobias frowned and said, 'Why is my father out the front of our house, loading suitcases onto the roof racks of our car? He never leaves the house by the front door. He usually uses our secret exit, the one the debt collectors don't know about.'

Tobias's father was frantically rushing back and forth between the house and the car, heaving overstuffed suitcases onto the car's roof, which was in danger of collapsing under the weight.

'Dad, what are you doing?' Tobias asked as he looked at the wobbly tower of suitcases.

Tobias's dad spun around, squealed, and leapt into the air. 'Oh,

Tobias, it's you.' He put his hand to his chest and took a lot of deep breaths. 'Quick, pack up all your stuff, we're moving. Maybe to Antarctica. Or anywhere that's as far away from Huggabie Falls as possible.' His eyes darted up and down Digmont Drive, and he scampered back inside.

Kipp, Cymphany and Tobias glanced at each other and had another one of those silent one-glance five-millisecond conversations. It went something like this:

Well so much for—

No one else getting scared before morning. I know. Tobias's dad is petrified.

Cymphany, it's not nice to interrupt someone, even if it is in a silent five-millisecond conversation. I mean you didn't do that before.

Hang on a second, what do you mean before? Did you guys have a silent five-millisecond conversation without me?

Sorry, Tobias, it was actually about you.

ABOUT ME?

Yes, it was about you eating flies.

Well, I never. It's not nice to talk behind someone's back, you know, even if it is a silent conversation held in a five-millisecond glance.

You're right. Sorry, Tobias.

Yes, sorry, Tobias.

Now, shall we have a real spoken conversation, because it appears we have a new problem. And although you can say a lot in a five-millisecond glance, this really might need some actual spoken words to sort out.

Good point. I second that.

I third that.

So Kipp, Tobias and Cymphany started talking, about the new problem, which was the fact that Tobias's dad seemed to be the latest victim of a scare ball. As they talked, they were unaware that, across the road, watching them from inside some bushes, some bushes that were just big enough to hide a grand piano, was a pair of tiny Brussels sprout eyes.

Definitely Not Chapter Thirteen

Please note: I have omitted chapter thirteen from this book and skipped straight to chapter fourteen, because thirteen is considered by some people to be an unlucky number. Now, I am not a particularly superstitious person, but my unlucky number is one million, four hundred and ninety-three thousand, nine hundred and seventeen. I find if you're going to have an unlucky number, it's better to have a really high one, as it is not going to come up very often.

Although, once when I was shopping at Mega-Mart-Super-Warehouse, I saw on my receipt that I was customer number one million, four hundred and ninety-three thousand, nine hundred and seventeen. I gasped, and at that exact moment I was attacked by an angry wombat. But I'm not sure if it was due to the fact that one million, four hundred and ninety-three thousand, nine hundred and seventeen really is an unlucky number, or more to do with the fact that a human gasp sounds exactly the same as a wombat declaration of war.

Whatever the case, there's already enough scariness going on in this book without me adding to it by having a chapter thirteen.

Don't worry, you won't miss anything, as I have taken all the words from chapter thirteen and put them in this chapter, and you'll find all the words from chapter fourteen in chapter fifteen, and so on. So when you come to the end of the book you'll have to subtract one to find the actual number of chapters in this book, if that's something you want to know.

But, when you think about it, even though this is called chapter fourteen, it is really chapter thirteen in disguise, so it's still just as likely to be unlucky, and there will probably be something super scary in this chapter like a spulling mistake or something—which is every author's worst nihgtmare.

Tobias's dad had something that was his worst nightmare: vacuum-cleaner salespeople, especially ones who come to your door and try to sell you a vacuum cleaner.

Tobias thought it was a pretty weird thing for his father to be petrified of. But he was pretty sure it had something to do with the time a vacuum salesperson came to their house, and his father signed up for a Super Sucker 5000, and because he didn't read the fine print on his contract he also inadvertently signed himself up for the Mars Habitation program, to be one of the first human settlers on Mars. This wouldn't have been such a problem, except for the fact that Tobias's dad was also quite afraid of red dirt.

Well, on the day that Kipp, Cymphany and Tobias had discovered the top-secret lab, and seen the scare balls that were scaring Huggabie Falls residents out of town, Tobias's dad had seen quite a lot of vacuum-cleaner salespeople walking up and down their street. And by quite a lot, I mean he had seen thousands of them. When Tobias's mum came home, she found her husband huddled in the corner, sobbing and clutching a wooden spoon for protection.

'Did you see?' Tobias's mum had said as she crawled into the house via the secret tunnel entrance. 'They're building a vacuum-cleaner-salespeople training centre next door.' She paused, seeing her petrified husband crouched on the floor. 'Oh, wait a minute, you don't like vacuum-cleaner salespeople, do you? Hang on a moment, why are you packing up all my yoga mats?'

'We're leaving town.' Tobias's dad had

mumbled. 'There are too many vacuum-cleaner salespeople here now. We're going to move somewhere where they don't have vacuum cleaners, or even carpets, like...' he paused, and thought hard for a moment. 'Like maybe Mars? Perhaps that habitation program I signed up for might be the best thing after all.'

Tobias, Kipp and Cymphany tried to explain to Tobias's dad, as they stood in the kitchen of the Treachery family's house, that the vacuum-cleaner salespeople weren't real, that they were hard-light holograms projected from a scare ball, and that Felonious Dark was on his way to fetch the Huggabie Falls police officer so he could arrest Felonious Dark Two and the top-hatted scientist and then all the scariness would stop.

But adults are known for not always listening to children, and this was one of those occasions. Tobias's mum just chuckled. 'You children have the wildest imaginations. I visited the House of Spooks this morning, and it was a hoot. The man in the lab coat and top hat, who insisted he wasn't a scientist, was lovely. He even gave me two collectible House of Spooks orbs free of charge. Now, where did I put them? That's strange. They were here a second ago. It's as if they grew legs and walked away.'

'The orbs are scare balls,' Tobias whimpered, getting scared all over again in case one of them projected a Brussels sprout with a very bad Scottish accent and a grand piano. 'And they *can* sprout legs.'

Tobias's mum's chuckle turned into a guffaw. 'Honestly, you children should write a book. This is hilarious.'

Tobias put his shaking hands on his hips and with a quavering voice said, 'Mum, what are you more scared of than anything else in this world?'

Tobias's mum gasped and began to quiver. 'Miniatures,' she said. 'You know when they make little cars and people and buildings and stuff out of plastic and then paint them so they look real. I swallowed a miniature Leaning Tower of Pisa once, and almost died. Miniature things send shivers up my spine. If things were meant to be that small, then they'd be that small! I never would have been able to swallow the real Leaning Tower of Pisa.'

Tobias's eyes were darting left and right anxiously, probably because he was hoping the scare ball contained his mum's fear and not his. 'Mum, I'm willing to bet that if you go outside now, you'll discover that on the other side of our house they are building a miniature world, or something very similar.'

'Oh, that is preposterous,' Tobias's mum laughed, as Tobias's dad bundled past her, heading out to the car with another packed suitcase. But Kipp, Tobias and Cymphany had very serious we're-not-joking expressions on their faces, and soon curiosity got the better of Tobias's mum and she went out into the front yard and peered over the side fence.

She came back inside moments later. Her

face was white and she looked like a ghost. 'I'll help you pack, Theodore,' she said to Tobias's dad, and she began shoving the television in a box.

'This is getting urgent,' Kipp said to Cymphany and Tobias, and they ran out of the house and towards the police station. 'We need to find Mr Dark, and the Huggabie Falls police officer quick smart, before the whole town is infested with those horrible scare balls.'

But when they got to the police station they found Felonious Dark sitting on the front fence staring at the ground with his shoulders slumped.

'Mr Dark,' Cymphany said. 'Did you find the police officer? We have to hurry. Tobias's parents are going to—'

But before she could finish Felonious Dark interrupted 'He's gone. He's left town.'

'Left town?' Kipp said. 'Like, gone to a police officers' conference or something, where they compare who has the shiniest badge?'

'No. Left town for good. Officer Snaildraw is terrified of alpacas,' Felonious Dark said, as a herd of alpacas wandered past the police station.

'This is crazy,' Tobias shouted. 'I don't care if Officer Snaildraw has left town, we have to save Conrad Creeps—he'll probably be scared to death before much longer, and I'm sure being scared to death is another thing he is scared of—and we have to find and deactivate all those terrifying scare balls.'

Tobias was being quite a lot braver than usual. He was scared of many things, but it seemed the thing he was scared of most of all, apart from Brussels sprouts with bad Scottish accents, was his family leaving Huggabie Falls.

'Although,' Tobias continued, 'I'm not sure how to stop scare balls. Do you think flyspray works on them? Anyway, you'll help us, won't you, Mr Dark?'

Felonious Dark looked up. 'Is that what a reformed evil person would do?'

'Definitely,' Cymphany said.

Felonious Dark stood up. 'All right, let's do it. I'm not going to get pushed around by some weird top-hat-wearing scientist and my brother, with his fancy long name. Let's go back to that House of Spooks and—'

Felonious Dark's face froze, and his eyes locked on something behind Kipp, Tobias and Cymphany, who all turned around in anticipation.

Standing in the middle of the road was a small tattered teddy bear, with one ear missing as if it had been chewed off, and one button eye hanging out of its eye socket by a piece of thread. The weirdest thing of all was that the teddy bear was smiling at them.

'Mr Puddles?' Felonious Dark said, his whole body trembling.

Kipp, Tobias and Cymphany spun back around. 'Mr Dark, who is Mr Puddles?' Tobias asked.

It took Felonious Dark a long time to answer. He didn't take his eyes off the bear. 'It's my...'

He paused and collected himself. 'I'd rather not say.'

Cymphany looked at Felonious Dark's face. 'Mr Dark, are you scared of that cute little bedraggled bear?'

'Don't be ridiculous,' Felonious Dark said, still not taking his eyes off the teddy bear. 'I'm not scared of Mr Puddles. I'm way beyond scared. I'm petrified.'

'But why?' asked Kipp.

'Did I mention I'd rather not say?' Felonious Dark said. 'But the last time I saw Mr Puddles was when I imprisoned him in chains and mailed him to Tunisia. And now he has found his way back, somehow.'

Tobias grabbed Felonious Dark's arm and shook it. 'No he isn't. Snap out of it, Mr Dark. Mr Puddles is not real. He's just a hard-light hologram.'

But at that moment, Mr Puddles took a step, and then another one. And he slowly walked towards them.

'Sorry, children,' Felonious Dark said as calmly as he could. 'Real or not, I'm terrified of that bear. You're on your own.' And he sprinted off down Digmont Drive screaming hysterically. The small bear turned to look at Kipp, Tobias and Cymphany, and his little teddy-bear eyebrows formed a ferocious V-shape. He sneered evilly at them, before leaping onto the back of a passing alpaca and galloping after Felonious Dark.

A second later, a scare ball, which was obviously the scare ball powering and projecting Mr Puddles, galloped past on the back of another alpaca.

Kipp, Tobias and Cymphany stared down the street in shock. Finally Tobias said, 'Wow, Mr Puddles and the evil Brussels sprout with the very bad Scottish accent should get together and go grand piano shopping or something.'

Cymphany raised a curious eyebrow at Tobias. 'Why?'

Tobias shrugged. 'I'm just guessing they'd have a lot in common.'

15

A Surprisingly Good Substitute

After the slightly weird experience, even by Huggabie Falls' particularly weird standards, of watching an evil hard-light hologram teddy bear chasing Felonious Dark on the back of an alpaca, Kipp, Tobias and Cymphany headed over to Cymphany's house, which was nearby on, unsurprisingly, Digmont Drive.

They found the house surrounded by a circle of geese. 'I'm going to take a wild guess,' Tobias said to Cymphany. 'That someone in your family is scared of geese.'

It was at precisely that moment that a shriek from above made them look up to the chimney on top of Cymphany's house, and they saw Cymphany's dad clinging to the top of it. 'We're moving,' he yelled. 'One of the main reasons I wanted to move to Huggabie Falls in the first place was that it didn't have a local goose population.' He jabbed a trembling finger at

the geese. 'Does that look like no local goose population to you?'

Cymphany began scanning the ground. 'We need to find the scare ball that's projecting all these geese and turn it off. If they can be turned off.'

'Seriously,' Tobias said. 'We should at least *try* some flyspray.'

Cymphany and Kipp gave him an as-if look.

They searched for the scare ball in the bushes in Cymphany's front yard, under rocks and in the letterbox, even in Cymphany's satchel, in case it had snuck in there. But their job was made very difficult by the geese, which kept flapping their wings and charging and snapping at them.

Kipp looked worried. 'I wonder if my parents have been scared by the scare balls too. Hopefully they're not packing the car to leave Huggabie Falls.'

Cymphany cupped her hands around her mouth and called up to her dad. 'Dad, we're going over to Kipp's. Don't go anywhere.'

'Go anywhere?' Cymphany's dad forced out a petrified squeak. 'I only wish our chimney was taller—then I'd go further up it. When your mother gets home tell her I'm having my dinner up here tonight. She should be back soon. She was just going to stop off and check out the House of Spooks. I popped in there this morning. It's wonderful. Lot of warning signs, though.'

'This is *not good*,' said Kipp. 'We have to get to my place now.'

When Kipp, Tobias and Cymphany arrived at Kipp's place they found everything was normal. Or as normal as things can be when both your parents are invisible.

'Have we been scared?' Kipp's mum's voice said, moments later, repeating Kipp's question. 'No, but we were just about to watch a scary movie.'

Kipp gasped. 'Did it come out of a small metal ball with spider legs?'

Even though Kipp couldn't see his mum's

face, she sounded like she was frowning. 'Ah...
no, it came from the movie shop.'

'Are you scared of movie shops, Ms Kindle?'
Tobias blurted out. 'Did the movie shop come
out of a small metal ball with spider legs? Did
the ball come from the House of Spooks?'

Kipp's mum laughed. 'The House of Spooks?
That new attraction? They were giving out free
tickets at the supermarket the other day. I went
there for a look this morning.'

'Did anyone give you a metal ball?' Cymphany
asked. 'Where is the ball?' she demanded, taking
a can of flyspray from her satchel, because it
was worth a try, and making Kipp and Tobias
amazed once again that Cymphany seemed to
have absolutely *everything* in that satchel.

Now Ms Kindle sounded concerned. 'No one
gave me a metal ball. Are you feeling all right,
Cymphany? And I'm not so sure you should be
carrying a can of flyspray around with you. It
could be dangerous.'

Cymphany stayed on guard for a moment,

but it soon become obvious the only thing her can of flyspray was going to be good for was spraying flies, and there were none of those about. She popped the can back in her satchel. 'Sorry, Ms Kindle,' she said. 'I might have got a little bit carried away. I think it's time for me to go home to my family, and the geese.'

And because everything seemed to be perfectly normal at Kipp's house, Cymphany and Tobias said goodbye and went home to their own terrified parents.

At school the next day, Kipp held up a poster. 'What do you think of this?' he said.

The poster was for a Nothing-Scary-Here-at-All party. Cymphany and Tobias had already seen it, many times, because it was plastered all over Huggabie Falls. Not that there were many people left in town to see the posters—the streets were getting more and more deserted by the hour.

The classroom Kipp, Tobias and Cymphany

sat in was similarly deserted. Kipp, Cymphany and Tobias were three of only five students in class. The other two students were Ug Ugg (the brainiac eleven-year-old troll, whose biggest fear was probably missing school, so it was no surprise he was there) and Lemonade Limmer. Lemonade was a time-traveller, who hadn't yet heard about the unbelievably scary thing that was happening in Huggabie Falls, because yesterday she had been in the year 1845. Their teacher, Mrs Turgan, had not shown up at all, and they wondered if she was still a pencil sharpener in the drawer, but no one dared take a look.

Cymphany took the 'Nothing Scary Here at All' party poster from Kipp, and read it out loud:

'At the House of Spooks we usually spend all our time trying to scare people. But considering all the unbelievably scary stuff that's going on in town, we want to give Huggabie Falls residents a nice place to get away from all the scariness,

and we promise there will be nothing scary at our party tonight, at all. And free popcorn.'

Cymphany looked closely at the picture of a very unscary unicorn holding flowers on the poster and screwed up her face. 'Why would the House of Spooks, which we know is behind all the scaring, be holding a Nothing-Scary-Here-at-All party?'

Tobias shrugged. 'Well, I think we'd better go and get some free popcorn...errr, I mean go and find out.'

'Somehow, I doubt

there is going to be any free popcorn,' Kipp said. 'But I'm sure the top-hatted scientist is definitely up to something.'

Tobias's jaw dropped. 'You mean the poster is *lying* about the free popcorn?' He slumped back in his seat. 'That's false advertising! Somebody should do something about the top-hatted scientist and the House of Spooks.'

'I've got it.' Cymphany clicked her fingers. 'I bet I know what Mr Dark Two and the top-hatted scientist are up to. It's probably taking too long to get the scare balls distributed to everyone in Huggabie Falls, but if you get the whole town together in one place...'

Kipp nodded. 'Then they can unleash the rest of the scare balls. It will be a mass-scaring event. The Nothing-Scary-Here-at-All party will soon become the Everything-Scary-Here party.'

'But I still don't understand,' Tobias said. 'Why did they lie about the free popcorn. I mean, that's just mean.'

Cymphany blinked at Tobias. 'Yes, Tobias.

We already know they are mean—they kidnapped Conrad Creeps.'

'I still don't understand,' Kipp said, 'why the top-hatted scientist didn't give my mum a scare ball.'

'Just be thankful he didn't,' Tobias said. 'My dad made my mum and me help him dig a moat around our house last night, so the vacuum-cleaner salespeople couldn't reach our front door. And we're leaving Huggabie Falls forever, straight after the Nothing-Scary-Here-at-All party tonight. We would have left today, but my dad loves free popcorn almost as much as I do.'

'Tobias is right,' Cymphany said to Kipp. 'Just be thankful neither of your parents have got a scare ball yet. My parents said I could say goodbye to everyone at the Nothing-Scary-Here-at-All party, and then they will pick me up on their way out of town.'

Kipp sighed. 'By tomorrow we could all be living in different towns.'

They sat in silence, absorbing the grimness of this thought.

Tobias looked very sad. 'I don't know what I'll do without you guys.'

'You won't have to do anything without us,' Cymphany said, jumping to her feet. 'Whatever Mr Dark Two and the top-hatted scientist are planning for tonight's party, we're going to stop it.'

Tobias and Kipp could see the look of determination in their friend's eyes, and it must have filled them with determination too, because they nodded. 'And,' Tobias said, 'at the very least we'll get some free popcorn.'

Cymphany's look of determination turned into a look of annoyance. 'Tobias, for the last time, I *really* doubt there is going to be any free popcorn.'

Tobias sighed. 'Oh, yeah, that's right. Wow, there's mean, and then there's lying-about-free-popcorn mean.'

Soon Cymphany and Tobias were so busy arguing about whether false free-popcorn advertising was worse than kidnapping someone and scaring people, and Kipp was so busy wondering when they would stop, that none of them noticed when an adult entered the classroom.

It wasn't Mrs Turgan, who was either still a pencil sharpener or had been scared out of town too.

I think it would fair to assume, as I did, that the adult entering the room and placing his briefcase on the desk at the front of the class was a substitute teacher. But, then again, it is dangerous to assume anything, particularly in Huggabie Falls, where weirdness and coincidences are quite normal.

When Kipp, Tobias and Cymphany looked up, they jumped in alarm, because standing at the front of the class, smiling in a sneering evil way, was Felonious Dark Two.

They could tell it was Felonious Dark Two because he stood with the sort of arrogant confidence that only a person with a name three letters longer than his next-longest-named sibling can stand.

'Hello, children,' he said. 'As you would have already assumed, if you are reckless enough to assume something in Huggabie Falls, I am your substitute teacher.'

'About time,' Ug Ugg said, and he flipped open his textbook and straightened his bow tie. 'We've missed nine minutes and nineteen seconds of valuable learning time already.'

Felonious Dark Two smiled and opened his briefcase. 'Before we start,' he said. 'I've got some presents I want you children to take home to your parents.' He removed two metal balls from his briefcase and placed them on the desk.

Kipp, Tobias and Cymphany gasped and recoiled.

Ug Ugg, on the other hand, bounded up to the front of the class.

'Don't do it, Ug,' Kipp said, and he jumped up. 'They're scare balls.'

Ug frowned at him, picking up a metal ball. 'I always listen to teachers. Maybe you should try it. You might get better marks.'

Cymphany's whole body jerked. 'Hey! I get *great* marks.'

Lemonade also collected her scare ball. Tobias opened his mouth to tell her to stop, but she held up her hand. 'It's okay, Tobias. I know this is a scare ball. I've already lived this week three times, and I know how this is all going to end.'

'Do you?' Tobias said. 'Can you tell us? It would be really great for my anxiety right now.'

'But that would ruin all the fun.' Lemonade smiled mischievously, lobbing the scare ball into the air and catching it, before sauntering back to her seat.

Tobias shook his head. 'What is the point of having a time-travelling kid in your class, if she won't tell you what happens in the future?'

Kipp didn't hear Tobias, as he was busy glaring at Felonious Dark Two. 'We know who you are,' he said.

Felonious Dark Two chuckled. 'Oh, really? Well congratulations. But that won't help you.'

'Why are you trying to scare everyone out of Huggabie Falls?' Cymphany asked.

Felonious Dark Two laughed. 'I'm afraid I've seen too many action movies where the diabolical evil genius is stupid enough to reveal his plan to the heroes. That would be the sort of thing my brother would do, but it's not really his fault he's stupid—he has three fewer letters in his name than I have. No wonder he had to become reformed.'

Tobias shook his head. 'I think you guys put too much importance on the number of letters in a person's name. Does that really matter?'

'Of course it matters,' Felonious Dark Two roared. 'All the greatest people in history have longer names than their siblings.'

Kipp blinked. 'Anyway, why are you here? To hand out more scare balls?'

Felonious Dark Two smiled. 'Isn't it obvious why I'm here?'

Cymphany turned to Felonious Dark Two, with a look as if to say, not really. Then she must have decided that the look wasn't enough, because she said, 'Not really.'

Felonious Dark Two laughed again. 'I'm a substitute teacher.'

'You are?' Kipp spluttered.

'The best long-named substitute teacher ever,' Felonious Dark Two said. 'Being an evil assistant to the top-hatted scientist is a great job, but teaching is my real passion. So if you'll open your textbooks to page ninety-three, we'll get started.'

So Kipp, Tobias and Cymphany, feeling more than a little bit bewildered, opened their textbooks to page ninety-three, and Felonious Dark Two began teaching the class. All things considered, he was actually a very good teacher. Not a single student got turned into an artichoke, like they often did when Mrs Turgan was teaching them, and they learnt a lot about long-named people who had changed the world, which was actually quite interesting.

When the bell rang, Felonious Dark Two

said, 'Unfortunately I won't see you tomorrow, children, as you will all have left Huggabie Falls by then. See you at the party tonight, though, I hope. It's going to be a scream.'

'That really was the best morning at school we've ever had,' Cymphany said to Tobias and Kipp as they walked to lunch. 'I can't believe the longest word in the English language contains 189,819 letters. And you know what, I think Mr Dark Two is right, it really is the best word. It's a shame we can't have Mr Dark Two as a teacher all the time.'

Kipp's eyebrows shot up. 'Cymphany! Mr Dark Two is working with the top-hatted scientist to scare everyone out of Huggabie Falls.'

'But look,' Cymphany said. 'He drew little smiley faces on my test. I mean, our tests end up covered in ox saliva when Mrs Turgan marks them.'

Tobias chewed on his lip thoughtfully. 'How are we going to stop Mr Dark Two and the top-hatted scientist, and destroy the scare balls, and destroy that machine, and rescue Conrad Creeps? Officer Snaildraw has left town, Mr Dark has been chased off by a weird old teddy bear, and no adults will listen to us.'

Cymphany sighed. 'Look, we've been in worse situations.'

'We have?' Kipp and Tobias said in unison. 'When?'

Cymphany stopped. 'Errr...' she said. 'We were chased by blood-sucking bats, attacked by vegetarian piranhas and, oh yeah, I was turned into a baby hippopotamus.'

Kipp nodded. 'But did you come face to face with your greatest fear?'

The look on Cymphany's face gave Kipp his answer. She was suddenly as white as milk.

'The top-hatted scientist made a scare ball for Tobias,' Kipp continued, 'and he's probably going to make one for each of us soon. I don't know about you, but I *definitely* don't want to see my greatest fear.'

'Actually, you're right,' Cymphany said. 'This is as bad as it's ever been.'

Tobias sighed. 'If only we could get an adult to listen to us. I mean, even that woman who runs the "We Always Listen" advice line wouldn't listen. I think she was lying when she said she'd turned deaf.'

And suddenly Cymphany stopped dead—which is to say she stopped abruptly, not to say that she actually died on the spot, which would have been quite horrifying.

'Wait a minute,' Cymphany said, as a smile spread across her face. 'I know an adult who can help us. But we will have to risk our lives to get to him.'

Kipp looked closely at Cymphany's face. Then a matching smile spread across his face. 'Are you thinking what I'm thinking?' he said.

Cymphany nodded, and then they both turned to Tobias.

Tobias studied their faces. 'Umm...you guys might be thinking the same thing, but I'm not sure I am. Because I'm still thinking about the unfairness of advertising free popcorn when you have no intention of providing it.'

So Kipp and Cymphany told Tobias who they were thinking of, and Tobias agreed it was an excellent plan, even if they had to risk their lives to reach the person they were now all thinking of.

The Nothing-Scary-Here-at-All Party

Now readers of this story might be slightly annoyed, that I, as storyteller, did not reveal in the last chapter the identity of the person Cymphany, Kipp and Tobias were thinking of, or why they had to risk their lives to get to him.

The reason I did not reveal this is because I was using a storytelling technique we storytellers use called 'building suspense'. It's the same reason that when you are watching a movie, and the movie's hero is hanging off a cliff, and the movie's villain is slowly stepping on each of the hero's fingers one by one, that right when the villain's boot is coming down on the hero's last finger, and the hero is surely about to plummet to a gruesome death that the movie will suddenly cut to a break, and you will be forced to spend five agonising minutes watching ads about new model four-wheel drives, low-fat cheese and a new television show about a Saint Bernard and a disgraced down-on-his-luck detective who team up to solve crimes, called *Paw and Order.*

I personally have always been against this sort of despicable suspense-building, although *Paw and Order* has become my all-time favourite television show. But now that I am a storyteller myself, I can see its usefulness. So I will skip past Kipp, Tobias and Cymphany going to visit the person they knew would listen to them, and jump straight to the Nothing-Scary-Here-at-All party.

The lawns surrounding the House of Spooks had been transformed into a fairground, complete with sideshows and rides and men in brightly coloured suits waving their arms and bellowing, 'Step right up, step right up,' and there was even a giant ferris wheel. Kipp and Cymphany weaved through the crowd, dodging balloons and teetering towers of fairy floss on sticks. They saw Tobias bounding towards them, holding a red-and-white-striped bucket. He had a huge beaming smile on his face.

'They *do* have free popcorn,' he said, enthusiastically scooping a handful out of the bucket. 'I never should have sent that complaint letter. This is great.'

'Tobias,' Cymphany said sharply. 'Don't forget why we're here. We have to save Conrad Creeps and stop the top-hatted scientist and Mr Dark Two before they...actually, I don't know know what diabolical thing they've got planned, but we have to stop them and save Huggabie Falls.'

'You mean stop them from holding a great party?' Tobias said. 'Did you see the bouncy castle over there? It's a full-size replica of Buckingham Palace!'

'It is peculiar,' Kipp said, looking around. 'We thought the top-hatted scientist and Mr Dark Two's plan was to scare everyone out of town, but this party seems to be doing the exact opposite.'

Tobias nodded. 'It's true. My dad was just saying before how much fun he was having, and how maybe he was a bit hasty in deciding to leave Huggabie Falls.'

'My dad said the same thing,' Cymphany said. 'He's having so much fun on that Spinmaster 10,000 ride over there, he seems to have forgotten all about the geese.'

Kipp looked at the party goers, laughing and enjoying themselves. There was even a giant hot-air balloon floating above the party that had 'Party Your Fears Away' emblazoned on it. 'I don't understand,' Kipp said. 'Why haven't my parents got scare balls? What are the top-hatted scientist and Mr Dark Two up to? I want to get back inside the House of Spooks and find out.'

'Inside the House of Spooks?' Tobias said warily, staring up at the creepy, spiderweb-covered house.

'Look,' said Cymphany pointing at a little window that was open. 'That little window is open. We could sneak in that way.'

'Or,' Tobias said, 'we could do something much less dangerous and stay out here and keep enjoying the free popcorn.'

Cymphany shot a fierce look at him. 'Tobias, don't forget about the Brussels sprout with the very bad Scottish accent—he's still after you, and he seems to have an unlimited supply of grand pianos.'

Tobias glanced about nervously. 'I was hoping the power in his scare ball had ran out,' he said hopefully, 'Or maybe...hey, what's that noise?'

'It sounds like whimpering,' Kipp said.

They followed the noise to a row of portaloos. When Cymphany saw them she stiffened and took a step backwards, obviously still a bit traumatised by her encounter with the Tyrannosaurus Rex. Kipp stepped up to the portaloo that was emitting the sound. He pressed his ear to the door.

'Mr Dark?' he said, knocking.

The whimpering stopped, and they heard the sound of a bolt sliding across. The portaloo door opened a crack and one of Felonious Dark's fearful darting eyes peeked out.

'Mr Dark?' Cymphany said, stepping forward. 'Are you okay?'

'Is he out there?' Felonious Dark whispered.

Kipp, Tobias and Cymphany looked around. 'Who?' Tobias asked.

'Who do you think?' Felonious Dark said. 'Mr Puddles.'

Kipp, Tobias and Cymphany scanned the rides and sideshows.

'There.' Kipp pointed. There was a gasp behind them and the portaloo door slammed shut again, followed by the sound of the bolt sliding back into place.

Tobias and Cymphany followed Kipp's pointing finger to see Mr Puddles standing at a sideshow where you shot water guns at rows of rubber ducks. With his little padded hands, Mr Puddles was holding a...

'That's weird.' Tobias rubbed his chin. 'If that's a water-gun sideshow, why is Mr Puddles holding a bow and arrow?'

Kipp had already worked out why, which is probably why he was running in the opposite direction. 'Quick!' he screamed. 'We've got to get to that window and sneak inside the House of Spooks.'

Tobias and Cymphany looked at each other and back at Mr Puddles, who had removed an arrow from the quiver on his back, spun around and pulled the arrow back in the bow. Without a moment's hesitation he shot it high into the air, and Tobias and Cymphany watched it fly up and up, headed straight for the giant hot-air balloon floating over the party. And suddenly Tobias and Cymphany were racing after Kipp, because

they had probably worked out, like Kipp already had, what was about to happen.

The arrow hit the balloon, and the balloon popped. And from inside it exploded thousands of scare balls. They rained down on the party, and as soon as they hit the ground they sprouted their little spider legs and began to open, projecting their unbelievably scary contents.

Within seconds the Huggabie Falls residents at the fair—who only moments ago had been laughing and chatting and cheering, and munching on free popcorn—were all wailing and screaming in fear.

17

Cymphany's Drawing

The screams of the Huggabie Falls residents became muffled and distant as Kipp, Tobias and Cymphany snuck along dark passageways inside the House of Spooks. Their progress was slow, as they had to crawl low past all the warning signs to avoid being detected by the hidden surveillance cameras in the i's, but eventually they found their way back to the secret lab.

'There's no one here,' Kipp said, looking around. From one of the hallways leading off the secret lab a voice floated: 'Kipp?'

Kipp's eyes spread wide. 'Is that you, Mum?' he said as he ran down the hallway.

Tobias and Cymphany looked at each other. 'What are Kipp's parents doing in here?' Cymphany asked.

Tobias shrugged, and they ran after Kipp and into another large round room. This one was lined with doorways blocked with vertical steel bars, and behind the bars were small stone-walled cells.

To Tobias and Cymphany's immense surprise—as he had been running in front of them just a second ago—Kipp was standing in one of these doorways *behind* the steel bars.

'Kipp,' Cymphany cried, and she grabbed the bars, looking up and down and left and right for a latch to open them. She tried to shake them, but they wouldn't budge. 'How did you get in there?'

Kipp was trying to jiggle the bars. 'The bars came crashing down as soon as I ran into this small room.'

'I couldn't warn him in time,' said a voice from nearby. Kipp, Tobias and Cymphany spun around. In one of the opposite cells, Conrad Creeps was peering out. And in the cell beside him was Kipp's little sister, Kaedy.

The voice Tobias and Cymphany had just heard seemed to be coming from Kaedy's cell, but not from Kaedy. And now another voice from that cell, still not Kaedy, said, 'We tried to alert him. But now we're all trapped in these cells.'

Tobias and Cymphany looked at each other. They knew those voices. 'Is that you, Mr and

Mrs Kindle?' Tobias asked.

Kaedy rolled her eyes. 'Derr, great guess, genius. I mean, how many other invisible people are there in Huggabie Falls?'

'The top-hatted scientist offered us a free ride on the House of Spooks ghost train, while the party was going on,' Mr Kindle's voice said. 'But the train ended up in here. Conrad has told us what's been going on: how the top-hatted scientist and Felonious Dark are trying to scare everyone out of Huggabie Falls.'

Conrad Creeps's head dropped. 'It's all my fault,' he said. 'And to make matters worse, I'm scared of cells.'

'It's weird,' Mrs Kindle's voice said. 'I thought Felonious Dark was reformed.'

'Actually, it's not Felonious Dark,' Tobias said. 'It's his identical triplet brother.'

'Pardon?' Mr Kindle said. 'Did you say identical *triplet* brother.'

'It's not important right now,' Cymphany said. 'What is important right now is how we get you out of here.'

'You have to go for help,' Mrs Kindle said. 'Before you are captured too.'

'I'm afraid there's no one left to help you,' said the top-hatted scientist, entering the large round room with Felonious Dark Two right behind him. 'Our little scare-ball party has scared everyone out of Huggabie Falls.'

Cymphany put her arm in front of Tobias in a protective manner, and stepped back away from the top-hatted scientist and Felonious Dark Two. 'What are you going to do?' she asked. 'Capture us too?'

The top-hatted scientist laughed. 'No, you are free to go. We are not kidnappers.'

'Ummm...' Mr Kindle's voice said. 'There are five people in cells in this room who would disagree with that.'

The top-hatted scientist ignored the comment, and Cymphany and Tobias took another step backwards. Cymphany's eyes darted to the only doorway that didn't have bars

on it or the top-hatted scientist and Felonious Dark Two standing in front of it. Her eyes met Tobias's and they gave each other a quick nod, as if to say, on the first chance we get, we'll run through that door, and hopefully it won't be another cell, but a way out.

As this quick nod was happening, the top-hatted scientist continued talking. 'We haven't kidnapped you, Mrs Kindle. We've just offered you an all-expenses-paid holiday here in the House of Spooks. It's an offer you cannot refuse. And after we have finished with our plan, you will all be released without harm.'

'And what is your plan?' Kipp asked. 'The last time a scientist was in Huggabie Falls, she was trying to turn everyone normal, and now you're trying to make everyone leave. Why?'

The top-hatted scientist smiled. 'I'm glad you asked. 'Our plan is—'

'Ahem.' Felonious Dark Two cleared his throat. 'It's not really a good idea to tell these children our plan. These particular children have been known to foil a good evil-scientist plan.'

The top-hatted scientist shot Felonious Dark Two a dark look. 'But I want to tell them. It's such a great plan. And it's not like there is anything they can do about it. My plan is completely foolproof.'

'That may be,' Felonious Dark Two said, 'but let's keep the plan to ourselves, just in case—'

'Need I remind you, Dark Two,' the top-hatted scientist said sternly, 'that you have a performance review coming up soon.'

Felonious Dark Two opened his mouth, then shut it again and rolled his eyes, as if to say, I really hope I get a chance to say I told you so later on, and a pay rise.

'So,' the top-hatted scientist continued. 'My predecessor—whom you just mentioned, and whom I understand you called the creepy scientist, but whose actual name is Agatha—did want to eliminate weirdness from this town. But I want to harness the weirdness. I've worked out a way to put the weird things in this town to good use. There's a bottomless hole in this town, which could solve all the world's waste-disposal problems. There's a reality rift in this town. I'm not sure what that is exactly, but it sounds very powerful. A man who can do anything, literally *anything*, in three minutes. And just the other day, I saw a real-life dragon. A dragon!'

'That's Burney,' Tobias said. 'Whatever you do, don't play fetch with him. A kid did that once, and he accidentally burnt down the fire station, which left no one to put out the fire, because...well, the fire station was on fire.' Tobias paused. 'I think it's still on fire, actually.'

'See what I mean,' the top-hatted scientist said. 'If I could harness the power of these weird things, think of all the good I could do for myself...err, I mean for the world. I hear there is even a girl who can time travel in your class.'

'So you're planning to capture Lemonade Limmer too?' Cymphany scowled.

'Well, no,' the top-hatted scientist said, and

he grimaced. 'She's actually living three years ago now, so we would've had to have captured her before we came up with this plan, which would have been difficult, even for me.'

Cymphany scowled. 'So you thought you'd scare everyone out of town so that no one would be left to stop you.'

Kipp sighed. 'Except me and my family,' he said. 'Because you want to be able to study our invisibility I suppose.'

The top-hatted scientist clicked his fingers. 'You kids are pretty smart. The first thing I want to do is to master invisibility, because it's crucial to my plan to conquer the world...err, I mean my plan to do good in the world. But don't worry'— he smiled at Kipp—'once we've worked out how to extract your family's invisibility, we'll let you all go, I promise.'

Kipp gripped the bars. 'Why have you got your hand behind your back? Have you got your fingers crossed?'

The top-hatted scientist jumped, quickly

whipping his hand out from behind his back. 'Of course not,' he yelped.

Then he paused for a moment. 'Okay, let me rephrase that,' he said. 'Once we've worked out how to extract your family's invisibility, we'll *probably* let you all go. But you two'—he turned back to Cymphany and Tobias—'we have no interest in extracting the power of standing on a slight lean or being treacherous, so you can go, and, like I said, everyone has been scared out of town now, so you won't find anyone to help you stop us. It's impossible.'

Felonious Dark Two took a deep despondent breath. 'I don't think you should have told them our *entire* plan,' he said.

'Remember that holiday,' the top-hatted scientist sneered, 'that you've got booked. I can still reject your leave request you know. The form hasn't been processed yet.'

'We're not leaving,' Cymphany said firmly. 'Not so you can do weird experiments on our friend and his family and poor Conrad.'

'Actually, I'm quite scared of experiments,' Conrad said.

Tobias nodded, sucking in a lungful of courage. 'There's no way we're leaving.'

The top-hatted scientist chuckled. 'We'll see about that.'

He and Felonious Dark Two stepped aside and a Brussels sprout with a grand piano under its arm stepped into the room.

'Nice ta see ye again, numpties,' the Brussels sprout said with a very bad Scottish accent.

Tobias gasped in fear, but it was the creature standing beside the Brussels sprout that made everyone else's eyes bulge and their faces fill with horror—and probably Kipp's parents' faces too, although no one could tell because they were invisible and this made it impossible to see their faces fill with anything, but the sound of two sharp gasps came from their cell.

Cymphany's face, which everyone could see, was twisting into all kinds of weird shapes. 'Oh dear,' she said. 'I was wondering when that would show up.'

Kipp gulped. 'Cymphany, what is...that?'

Cymphany shivered. 'When I was young I thought it was silly that kids were scared of stupid things like ghosts and the dark, and Brussels sprouts—no offence, Tobias.'

'None taken,' Tobias said, but while everyone else was looking at what Cymphany was looking at, Tobias wasn't taking his eyes off the Brussels sprout with the grand piano under its arm.

'So,' Cymphany continued, 'one day in class, when our teacher asked us to draw a picture of something that scared us, I drew the most absolutely terrifying creature I could imagine. And as you can see'—she gestured at the creature standing in front of them—'I did a pretty good job.'

'You can say that again,' Kipp stammered.

A rumbling growl from the most absolutely terrifying creature's throats reverberated around the room. It focused its nineteen eyes on them, and wiped the drool dripping off its fangs with one of its barb-covered tentacles.

It was so unbelievably scary that even Tobias stopped being scared of the Brussels sprout with the very bad Scottish accent and became scared of the most absolutely terrifying creature instead. He had to steady himself against Cymphany so he didn't faint.

'If you think it's scary now, wait till you see what's about to come out of that little door in its stomach,' Cymphany said, and she started running.

And when the doorway in the most absolutely terrifying creature's stomach opened and Tobias saw what came out, he started running too, so fast that he quickly overtook Cymphany.

18

Free Popcorn,
But Still a Bad Party

When the sun rose the next morning, Cymphany and Tobias lay exhausted on the shore of the bottomless lake. Their eyes were red, their clothes were tattered, and their arms were covered in scratches.

They'd been running through the bush all night, dodging and hiding from the most absolutely terrifying creature and the Brussels sprout with the very bad Scottish accent. At one point the forest floor was covered with pieces of smashed grand piano but, as they were all just pieces of hard-light holograms, after a while their power ran out and they evaporated. Unfortunately the Brussels sprout with the very bad Scottish accent and the most absolutely terrifying creature's power never seemed to run out.

'What a horrible night,' Tobias said, struggling to sit up. 'And, to make matters worse, we're lost.'

Cymphany sat up too. She rifled through her satchel for a few moments and pulled out a compass.

'Honestly,' Tobias said, amazed. 'I know I've joked about this before, but, *seriously*, is there anything you don't have in that satchel?'

Cymphany stood up and slowly turned around in a circle, looking carefully at the wavering needle on the compass. 'Well, I don't have a helicopter, which would be really useful right now.' She looked up, as if to check whether there was a big enough gap in the trees for a helicopter to fly through. 'Looks like we're going to have to walk. It's this way. South.'

They began to walk, but it wasn't long before Cymphany groaned. 'This is horrible. How can we can keep our greatest fears away? Those creatures don't give up. And our best friend and his family and Conrad Creeps are being held for evil scientific experiments, and I don't know what we can do to save them.'

Tobias sighed. 'Surely you've got something in your satchel that can help us win the day, or'—his empty stomach rumbled—'maybe a sandwich?'

Cymphany shook her head. 'It's too late. Right now, we've got about as much chance of beating the top-hatted scientist and Mr Dark Two as we have of finding sunken treasure on the bottom of the bottomless lake.'

Tobias frowned. 'But it's bottomless.'

Cymphany stared at him. 'Exactly.'

Tobias thought for a moment. 'Oh,' he said, forlornly.

Tobias was extra worried now. Cymphany was the one who never stopped coming up with plans and pulling useful items out of her satchel, even hours after he and Kipp were out of ideas. If she was giving up, then maybe things really were hopeless. He trudged despondently with Cymphany along the shore of the bottomless lake.

After a few moments Tobias heard a soft sobbing noise and then a wet sniffle. He put his hand on Cymphany's shoulder. 'There, there, Cymphany, don't cry. It's not over. I mean we can still...we haven't...there's still a chance we could...' Tobias squeezed his lips together to hold back his own tears. 'Oh, you're right, Cymphany, it's hopeless. Do you mind if I blubber along with you?'

Cymphany turned and stared at him. 'Tobias, what are you talking about? I'm not crying.'

Tobias looked up, sniffling himself now, and wiped a few loose droplets from his cheeks. He saw Cymphany had the same steely glare she always had. 'Well then, who is?' Tobias asked. 'I can still hear someone crying.'

Cymphany listened. 'Me too,' she said.

They looked through some bushes near the water's edge and saw Cymphany's most absolutely terrifying creature and the Brussels sprout with the very bad Scottish accent sitting on a grand piano. Nearby were two scare balls sitting on their folded spider legs. The most absolutely terrifying creature's shoulders were heaving up and down. Tears of acid were running down its cheeks and burning holes in the lid of the grand piano, while wet globs of snot were dribbling off its fearsome beak.

The Brussels sprout with the very bad Scottish accent looked up at them, and Tobias prepared to run. But the Brussels sprout didn't jump off the grand piano and get ready to throw it, he just huffed. 'Ah, away with ye. Do ye nae see we're nae doing any scaring just the noo. Do ye nae see how upset ye've made her?'

'How upset we've made her?' Cymphany

put her hands on her hips. 'You're the ones who have been chasing us all night.'

The most absolutely terrifying creature lifted her head. 'Well, what do you expect?' she snarled. 'When people see me, they run anyway, so I may as well chase them, otherwise I'd always be alone. I mean, do you have any idea what it's like, looking like I do? I can't do anything normal creatures do. Why did you have to draw me so terrifying?'

'Actually...' Cymphany looked startled. 'It was Conrad Creeps who imagined you.'

The creature sighed, bowing her yellow, boil-covered head. 'He just imagined the most unbelievably scary creature ever, just like you did when you were a kid.' More acid tears dripped off the most absolutely terrifying creature's face, leaving a few more holes in the piano lid. 'I mean, I've never had a friend.'

Cymphany opened her mouth to say something, and then closed it again when the Brussels sprout with the very bad Scottish accent chimed in. 'Aye, we're nae the bad guys here. He is.' He jabbed a leafy finger at Tobias. 'I'm only trying ta scare him off before he eats me.'

Tobias's mouth dropped open. 'I would never eat you.'

'Ha!' The Brussels sprout threw his head back. 'I bet ye would, first chance ye get, just like ye ate all ma brothers an' sisters.'

Tobias shook his head. 'I haven't eaten a Brussels sprout since I found out they have feelings. In fact, I used to take Mum's Brussels sprouts out of the pantry and set them free on our back lawn, that is'—Tobias looked unsure if he should finish his sentence—'until I found out the birds were eating them.'

'The birds!' The Brussels sprout with the very bad Scottish accent jumped up and went to pick up the grand piano. 'Ye monster!'

'Wait,' Tobias held out his hands. 'I promise I will never eat another Brussels sprout again. I feel terrible about all the ones I've already eaten. But I promise I won't ever eat another one. You don't have to keep throwing grand pianos at me.'

The Brussels sprout stared at Tobias with untrusting vegetable eyes.

'You can trust him,' Cymphany said to the Brussels sprout. 'Even though his surname is Treachery, Tobias is one of least treacherous and most trustworthy people you'll ever meet.'

The Brussels sprout with the very bad Scottish accent fixed his eyes on Tobias for a moment and then gave a tiny nod, as if to say, I trust him, for now, but if he steps out of line, I've still got plenty of grand pianos.

Cymphany stood beside the most absolutely terrifying creature, who was still sobbing. She took a handkerchief out of her satchel and handed it to her. 'And you can trust me, when I say that I'm happy to be your friend,' she said to the most absolutely terrifying creature.

The most absolutely terrifying creature's barnacle-encrusted eyes opened wide. 'Really?' her voice croaked. 'You're my first friend?' She blew her nose loudly into the handkerchief.

Cymphany nodded. 'What's your name?'

The most absolutely terrifying creature oozed a grin. 'Bugsplatter.'

Cymphany recoiled slightly, but then forced a smile. 'That's a lovely name,' she said.

Bugsplatter's face brightened. Her gills even flapped. 'You really think so?'

'Definitely.' Cymphany smiled, for real this time. 'And you're in luck. There are lots of weird things in Huggabie Falls. So you'll fit right in. You could have lots of friends.'

'More than one friend?' Bugsplatter seemed to jolt. 'That just seems greedy.'

'But if everyone is scared out of town, there won't be anyone left to be friends with,' Cymphany explained. 'So will you help us stop the top-hatted scientist and Mr Dark Two, and rescue Conrad Creeps and our best friend and his family?'

Bugsplatter nodded. 'I will help my first friend, and all my soon-to-be friends.'

'Only problem is,' Cymphany said, 'it's going

to take us ages to get back to Huggabie Falls.'

Bugsplatter put one of her giant crab claws to her green chin and thought for a moment. Then she said, 'Not really. I have wings folded into my shell, so I could fly us back.'

'Oh, I didn't even notice those,' Cymphany said as she peered at Bugsplatter's back. 'And what about you?' Cymphany said to the Brussels sprout. 'Will you help us too?'

'I've got a name, too, ye know,' the Brussels sprout said, in a very put-out way.

'Oh, sorry,' Cymphany said. 'How rude of me. What's your name?'

The Brussels sprout nodded and crossed his tiny arms. 'It's Brussels Sprout.'

No one said anything for a few seconds. 'Okay...' Cymphany said, slowly, as if to say, this is weird but then again it is Huggabie Falls. 'Will you help us, Brussels Sprout?'

Brussels Sprout rubbed his chin, just like Bugsplatter had a moment ago, which was quite a trick, as Brussels sprouts don't really have chins. 'Do these bad folks eat Brussels sprouts?'

'Definitely,' Cymphany said, nodding vigorously. 'Every day.' She did not also mention that many of the residents of Huggabie Falls regularly ate Brussels sprouts.

A mischievous grin appeared across Brussels Sprout's face. 'Den it's poundin' time.'

'But wait,' Bugsplatter said. 'Hasn't everyone been scared out of Huggabie Falls already? They're probably halfway to Antarctica by now.'

Cymphany shared a knowing grin with Tobias. 'Actually, we went and saw a person yesterday. Someone who could help us.' She took a deep breath. 'And, fingers crossed, or in Bugsplatter's case tentacles crossed, that person is doing what we asked him to do.'

19

What the Mystery Person
Was Asked to Do

Cymphany, Tobias and Brussels Sprout flew on
Bugsplatter's back all the way to the only road
out of Huggabie Falls, which was, of course,
called Digmont Drive. They reached the spot
where the road crossed a drawbridge over the
Huggabie Falls River. All the escaping Huggabie
Falls residents were stuck on the Huggabie
Falls side of this drawbridge, because the drawbridge
was up. And the drawbridge was up because
Mr Haurik's enormous ship, with the skull and

crossbones flag flying from the mast and the inbuilt four-storey caravan with the rooftop tennis court, was parked beneath it.

The residents of Huggabie Falls were standing on the riverbank, shouting and shaking their fists at Mr Haurik. Every few seconds Mr Haurik's head popped up from beneath the deck, and he smiled and waved apologetically. 'So sorry about this, me hearties. I think me thingamajig is broken, or maybe me dooberwacky is out of whack. Should have it fixed in a jiffy. *Arrrgh.*'

'Is that a pirate?' Bugsplatter asked, as they flew down and landed beside the angry mob.

'Careful what you say,' Cymphany said, as she, Tobias and Brussels Sprout climbed down to the ground. 'Mr Haurik hates any mention that he resembles those "murderous scavengers of the seas", as he calls pirates.'

Bugsplatter blinked. 'This town really is weird.'

Brussels Sprout had not taken his eyes off Tobias for the whole flight. 'Nae feeling a wee bit puckish, are ye, lad?'

Tobias threw up his hands. 'I keep telling you, I'm not going to eat you!'

Cymphany waved at Mr Haurik and mouthed, 'Thank you.'

Mr Haurik waved back. He had done what Kipp, Tobias and Cymphany had asked him to do yesterday, which was to delay everyone from leaving Huggabie Falls for as long as he possibly could. Kipp, Tobias and Cymphany had risked their lives to contact Mr Haurik by lighting a big fire on the shore of the bottomless lake and getting dangerously, eyebrow-singingly close to it as they used their school jumpers to cover the flames to send him a smoke signal.

Not far from the crowd of Huggabie Falls residents waiting to cross the drawbridge was a second crowd, which was made up of all the Huggabie Falls residents' greatest fears, and what a fearsome group they were: two-metre tall spiders, and snakes, and boogey men, and a pineapple holding a chainsaw, and even a cloud, because it seemed someone in Huggabie

Falls was scared of low-flying vapour-filled weather formations. Scuttling around on their little spider legs in between the feet, hooves and bellies of all the fearsome creatures were the scare balls, which were powering and projecting the creatures.

At the front of the crowd, Mr Puddles marched back and forth on his squelchy padded fabric feet, waving a cutlass above his head—where did he get a cutlass from, Tobias wondered—and bellowing, 'If they don't leave soon, we're going to get them!' And the crowd of fearsome creatures pumped their fists and claws and tentacles and flippers and scythes and balloons (that was the clown) in the air, and yelled, 'Yeah,'—except for the cloud, which instead made a *whiiiiiiiioooooooo* sound, which in cloud language means 'you betcha'.

'Tell that bathtub to stop staring at me,' Mrs Turgan screeched, ducking for cover behind a rock. Mrs Turgan wasn't a pencil sharpener any-more, but she had bits of pencil shavings in her hair. The bathtub in question wasn't staring at her, as bathtubs don't have eyes, but there was a rubber ducky floating in the bubbly water in the tub, and no matter how much the ducky bobbed about, its eyes stayed glued to Mrs Turgan.

Tobias wondered briefly why Mrs Turgan was still here, and why she hadn't just flown away, but then he saw that one leg of the bathtub was on top of Mrs Turgan's broomstick, pinning it to the ground, while it twisted and squirmed and tried to get free.

Cymphany's parents spotted her and made their way through the crowd. 'Cymphany, where have you been?' her mum said, and she grabbed Cymphany and looked her up and down. 'Are you okay? We have been worried sick about you.'

'We thought the geese had got you,' Cymphany's dad said as he looked towards the group of fearsome creatures, and particularly towards a group of geese—which were all giving him the evil eye. 'We're trying to escape from— *eurgh*...what is that?'

Cymphany smiled. 'Mum, Dad, this is Bugsplatter. She may look terrifying, but she's actually my friend. She's very nice.'

'I am,' Bugsplatter said. 'Although I get a bit grumpy when I'm hungry.'

'She can't be as scary as that amateur poet over there,' Cymphany's mum said. 'I'm staying as far away from him as possible.'

She pointed at a man wearing a beret and a cocktail jacket who was standing on the fringes of the fearsome creatures group. The man flourished his hand and said:

'To bee or not to bee,
That is the pollen.'

Cymphany's mum's face went green. 'I think I'm going to be sick. We have to get out of here.'

'Why has she got a door in her stomach?' Cymphany's dad pointed at Bugsplatter's stomach.

'Don't worry about that,' Cymphany said quickly. 'Dad, you have to lift me up onto your shoulders. There's something I have to tell the people of Huggabie Falls.'

'What, now?' Cymphany's dad glanced at the geese. 'Can't it wait till we are away from here, in a nice goose-free area?'

'And bad-poetry-free area,' Cymphany's mum added as she stuffed a handkerchief into one of her ears.

'Mum, Dad, it can't wait,' Cymphany said very firmly. 'Please, lift me up now. Huggabie Falls' future depends on it, and we have to rescue Conrad Creeps and Kipp and his family.'

'Wait.' Cymphany's mum turned away from the poet, full of concern. 'What happened to Kipp and his family?'

'I'll explain everything,' Cymphany said, 'if Dad hurries up and lifts me onto his shoulders.'

Cymphany's parents were a bit confused, but Cymphany's mum urged Cymphany's dad to lift Cymphany onto his shoulders, and be quick about it, and so that's what he did.

As Cymphany's dad hoisted Cymphany up

onto his shoulders, Tobias's family came over.

'Tobias, my boy,' Tobias's dad said. His eyes were bloodshot. 'We've got to leave this town. These vacuum-cleaner salespeople are multiplying by the second. And they've got a new model: the Super Sucker 6000. It's a whole 1000 better than the Super Sucker 5000. It's taking all my willpower not to buy it. But if I sign another contract, I could end up on Pluto!'

'It's okay, Dad,' Tobias said. 'Just listen to what Cymphany has to say.'

Tobias's dad squealed as a vacuum-cleaner salesperson with a clipboard and pen rocketed towards them, tapping her watch. 'Time is running out, Mr Treachery,' she said. 'I'm afraid the Super Sucker 6000 offer is only valid for another nineteen seconds.'

'Nineteen seconds!' Tobias's dad yelped, his signing hand involuntarily springing forward.

Luckily, before Tobias's dad could sign yet another contract he hadn't read properly—whose small print probably said he had to clean toilets in the Great Pyramid of Giza for the next fifty years—Cymphany, from up on her dad's shoulders, removed a megaphone from her satchel, put it to her mouth and began her speech.

'People of Huggabie Falls,' Cymphany's voice boomed through the mega-phone. 'You have been duped by a top-hatted scientist and Mr Dark's evil identical triplet brother, Felonious Dark Two.'

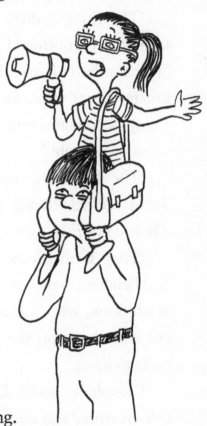

Felonious Dark nodded, as he seemed to have miraculously appeared out of no-where, as characters in books and movies often do when it's important for them to suddenly say something.

'It's true. My brother is very evil,' Felonious Dark said. Then his attention was distracted by something in the distance. 'Why is Gertrude hiding behind that bush?' He looked up in the sky. 'Ah, that's right. She is scared of low-flying, vapour-filled weather formations.'

'The things you're scared of are not real,' Cymphany continued her megaphone speech. 'The top-hatted scientist found out what your greatest fears were, and he tapped into Conrad Creeps's imagination to create the scariest versions of them.'

'The fears are just hard-light holograms,' Tobias added. 'Being projected by scare balls. They're not real.'

'They seem pretty real to me,' shouted Ms Suddlehoney, owner of Ms Suddlehoney's Wish Shop, who was afraid of sloths, and was currently lying on the ground while a sloth sat on her chest.

Cymphany nodded. 'I used to be scared of this creature,' she said, gesturing with her hand, the one that wasn't holding the megaphone, to Bugsplatter.

'What is that thing coming out of the door in its stomach?' yelled one Huggabie Falls resident.

'Is that a fish?' another resident asked.

'I think it's a camel,' said another. 'No... it's...'

'It's hideous,' yelled someone else.

Cymphany waved her hand frantically. 'It doesn't matter. What matters is I had no reason to be scared of her. Most of the time our fears are in our mind, and the things we're scared of aren't really scary at all, or they don't mean to be scary. Quite often it's not their fault that we're scared.'

Bugsplatter stepped forward. She cleared her throat and looked out across the crowd. 'Oh, I'm so nervous,' she squeaked. 'Get it together, Bugs,' she mumbled to herself. Then, she addressed the crowd. 'Do not judge me, for what you see on the outside. Inside, I'm not scary at all. Well, except for the thing behind the door in my stomach, but I'll keep that door closed. I don't want to scare anyone anymore.'

The crowd went silent. Bugsplatter wondered if this was the kind of pause that occurred before thunderous applause broke out.

Then someone put up their hand. 'What sort of a name is Bugsplatter anyway?'

Cymphany's mum looked blissfully happy. With handkerchiefs stuffed in both her ears, she hadn't heard anything.

Cymphany smiled. 'The point is, being scared of things is okay. Our fears are part of what makes us who we are. But we can't let our fears control us. We have to learn to accept them, maybe even embrace them. Look at us all: the top-hatted scientist and Mr Dark Two are using our fears to control us. We're all about to leave the town we love. And why?' Cymphany looked around, seemingly picking the closest thing to her and gesturing to it. 'Because of a teddy bear!'

Felonious Dark looked up. 'But Mr Puddles

is terrifying. He's always chasing me.'

Mr Puddles scoffed. He waved his arms and did a silly exaggerated voice. *'Mr Puddles is terrifying. He's always chasing me.* Give me a break. I'm not terrifying. I'm grumpy.' He shook his fist. 'And so would you be, if you hadn't had a good night's sleep in years. Do you think I wanted to stay awake night after night, just because you were scared of the dark?'

Tobias looked at Felonious Dark and then at Mr Puddles. 'Is anyone else confused? Mr Dark, what is going on?'

It took Felonious Dark a moment to answer. He took a big breath. 'When I was a child, I was scared of the dark. My parents put an old teddy, with an ear chewed off by the family dog, by my bed. They called him Mr Puddles. He was supposed to look after me and keep me company so I wouldn't get scared. And he did, for a long time, but he's a scary-looking bear. I started having nightmares that Mr Puddles was chasing me. I stopped being scared of the dark and started being scared of Mr Puddles. So my parents finally got rid of him.'

Mr Puddles huffed. 'How's that for gratitude.'

Cymphany frowned, lowering the megaphone so she could whisper to Felonious Dark. 'How long did Mr Puddles protect you, Mr Dark?'

Felonious Dark shrugged. 'About five or ten years I think.'

'Try twenty-one years,' Mr Puddles shouted.

Everyone was quiet for a moment.

'Does anyone else,' Tobias said, breaking the silence, 'think it's hilarious that Mr Dark was scared of the dark?' He chuckled until he noticed everyone was glaring at him. 'What?' he said. 'It *is* funny.'

Mr Puddles waved his padded paws. 'It's not funny. I had plans. I wanted to become an accountant. I wanted to go to university. But, you know who can't go to university? Teddy bears who have to babysit ungrateful kids who are scared of the dark—that's who. You ruined my life, Felonious Dark, and you never even apologised.'

The crowd fell silent. Felonious Dark opened his mouth, looking set to retort, but then he closed it again. 'I guess...' He shook his head. 'I guess, ummm, I never really thought about it like that.'

Mr Puddles crossed his stumpy teddy-bear arms and spun around so he faced away from Felonious Dark. 'Yes, well, thinking was never your strong point,' he muttered.

The silence continued, for quite a long time, before Felonious Dark finally said, 'I'm sorry.'

Mr Puddles turned his furry head slightly. 'You are?'

Felonious Dark nodded. 'Yes, I'm sorry.' He smiled and opened his arms out wide.

And Mr Puddles ran and dived into Felonious Dark's outstretched arms, giving him a mini bear hug.

Many of the Huggabie Falls residents and a few of the fearsome creatures sniffled and wiped their weeping eyes.

Cymphany raised her megaphone to her

mouth again. 'We can't allow the top-hatted scientist and Felonious Dark Two's plan to succeed. So if Mr Dark can make up with Mr Puddles, surely we all can make friends with our greatest fears. And then we can all go get our town back.'

Seeing Felonious Dark hugging Mr Puddles made the people of Huggabie Falls take a good hard look at their own greatest fears.

Tobias's dad slowly approached the group of vacuum-cleaner salespeople. 'Look,' he said, taking a deep breath. 'I want the new Super Sucker 6000, I really do, but I don't want a contract with hidden clauses.'

One of the vacuum-cleaner salespeople nodded and flipped to a new page on her clipboard. 'Ah, so you want one of our no-hidden-clauses contracts.'

Tobias's dad jumped with excitement. 'You have those?'

The vacuum-cleaner salespeople shared a laugh between themselves. 'Of course. We're not heartless monsters, except for Larry, over there, who is *actually* a heartless monster, which is Pogsley Pottlebrush's greatest fear.'

Larry, who was a rather large monster with a gaping hole in his chest where a heart usually should be, wiped a tear from his eye. 'I may not have a heart,' he sobbed, 'but I have lots of love to give.'

Pogsley Pottlebrush, who had been hiding from Larry behind a tree, stepped out, and put his hand to his chest. '*Awwww*,' he said—in the same way Kipp's mum always did when there was a miniature poodle on TV—'you poor thing.' He went over and gave the sobbing monster a hug. 'I can't believe I was ever scared of you. You're just a big crybaby, aren't you?'

Larry was bawling now. Waves of tears cascaded down his face. 'I can't even watch sad movies, unless I'm sitting in a boat.'

And the greatest fears reconciliations continued, with most people realising that the things they were scared of weren't really all that scary. Some people even started patting the little scare balls, which actually *purred* with delight.

And the bathtub let Mrs Turgan's broomstick free. Mrs Turgan sat on the edge of the bathtub, chatting to the rubber ducky. 'You know, maybe having a bath wouldn't be so bad. Maybe all these flies would stop hanging around me if I smelled a little more pleasant. And thank you for letting my broomstick go. Interesting fact: broomsticks aren't just used for flying, you can also use them to sweep up breadcrumbs.'

Even Cymphany's dad admitted that geese weren't so frightening, especially after Cymphany put her megaphone back in her satchel and told him the interesting fact that a single goose can eat up to a kilogram of grass a day. Cymphany's dad did a quick head count of the geese. 'Wow. I may never have to mow the front lawn again. Perhaps I should invite them to move in.'

Before long, the people of Huggabie Falls had their arms around their greatest fears, and everyone was laughing and joking.

Cymphany's mum finally took the handkerchiefs out of her ears. 'What's going on?' she asked. 'Did I miss something?'

She turned and saw the poet standing beside her, with a goofy grin on his face, and she was about to make a run for it, but the poet put up his hand to stop her and explained what had been happening.

And Cymphany's mum, keen to continue the spirit of reconciliation, gritted her teeth and allowed the bad poet to read her one of his poems. He began:

Poe-a-tree, poe-a-tree,
How I leaf thee.
Your roots dig into me,
Until I find the key.

When the bad poet had finished, Cymphany's mum blinked a few times, but she didn't look *totally* terrified.

The poet looked hopeful.

'Well, that was the worst thing I've ever heard,' Cymphany's mum said. 'It didn't even make sense.' The look of hope on the poet's face faded.

'But I'm still standing,' Cymphany's mum said, and she shrugged. 'I didn't faint or anything, this time.'

A smidgen of hope returned to the poet's face. 'Shall I recite another poem?' he said.

'Don't push your luck,' Cymphany's mum said. 'At least I'm not terrified of you anymore.'

The greatest fears love-fest continued, until Tobias's clapping hands got everyone's attention.

He stood with Cymphany, Bugsplatter and Brussels Sprout. 'It's great that we're all friends now and everything, but let's not forget it was the top-hatted scientist and Felonious Dark Two who caused all of this, and they also kidnapped Conrad Creeps and our friend Kipp Kindle and his family. I think it's time we paid them a little visit.'

The people of Huggabie Falls looked into the eyes of their greatest fears, and determined looks began to form. The greatest fears didn't much like being scary, and the Huggabie Falls residents didn't really like being driven out of Huggabie Falls, and there were two people to blame for all of it. Bugsplatter perfectly captured everyone's thoughts in one three-word sentence.

'It's payback time,' she chuckled.

20

Mocktails and the End of the Story

Felonious Dark Two and the top-hatted scientist sat on the porch of the House of Spooks, drinking celebratory mocktails.

'This mocktail is scrumptious,' Felonious Dark Two said as he took a slurp.

'The secret ingredient,' the top-hatted scientist said, chinking his glass with Felonious Dark Two's, 'is evilness.'

'*Ahhh*,' said Felonious Dark Two. 'And here I was thinking it was cinnamon.'

Trucks full of scientific apparatus were rolling into town in a rumbling line. The top-hatted scientist was about to commence his experiments. He was going to extract the weirdness from everything in the town, starting with the Kindle family's invisibility. He had a lot of other plans too, and one of them involved the Tuggenmeisters' inter-dimensional letterbox, which existed in every dimension simultaneously. You could put a letter in it and it would be read by an alternative version of yourself in an alternative dimension, and your other self could send you a letter back before you'd even posted the first letter. The top-hatted scientist was sure if he could open a portal to this other dimension, then he could rule the world, or become insanely rich.

The top-hatted scientist took in a deep satisfying lungful of air. 'With all the residents of Huggabie Falls scared out of town, no one can get in the way of my experiments to extract all the weirdness in Huggabie Falls. And I will become the most rich and powerful person in the world.'

He saw Felonious Dark Two raise an agitated eyebrow at him.

'Errr,' the top-hatted scientist said. 'I mean *we* will become the most rich and powerful *people* in the world.'

Felonious Dark Two smiled. He was already planning on pushing the top-hatted scientist into the other dimension, and closing the portal behind him, as soon as possible.

'So, Felonious,' the top-hatted scientist said. 'We have officially won. If someone was writing a book about all my adventures, then this glorious moment would be the end of it.'

But the top-hatted scientist should know, as all

good storytellers know, that a story is never over until the words 'the end' appear. Felonious Dark Two must have known this, and he must also have known it is dangerous to tempt fate by saying things like 'We have officially won', because he lowered his agitated eyebrow and raised his mocking eyebrow, and said, 'You know it's dangerous to tempt fate by saying things like that.'

The top-hatted scientist laughed so hard a bit of mocktail came shooting out of his nose. 'Don't be ridiculous, Dark Two. It's not like everyone in town is going to make friends with their greatest fears and come back to get—hey, what's that?'

The top-hatted scientist stood up, squinting down the road. Felonious Dark Two stood up too. A huge crowd was marching along Digmont Drive towards the House of Spooks, a crowd containing Huggabie Falls residents, arm-in-arm with their greatest fears.

The top-hatted scientist gulped as he turned

to Felonious Dark Two. 'Don't even think about saying, "I told you so".'

Felonious Dark Two looked back at the top-hatted scientist. 'Actually,' he said. 'There's never been a better time to say, "I told you so".'

21

Time Crystals and Lemonade

Felonious Dark Two was wrong, by the way, when he said there's never been a better time to say, 'I told you so'.

The absolute best time to say I told you so was officially recorded ten years earlier. It had started when Huggabie Falls resident Meta Morphosis was tipping time crystals down the kitchen sink and his wife, Merida, told him she didn't think that was a good idea.

Some readers out there might be wondering

what time crystals are. Put quite simply, they are crystals made up of time, and now that we've cleared that up, can we get on with the story, please?

Yes?

Good. It seems the time crystals mixed with some lemonade (which coincidentally is how Lemonade Limmer got her name) that had been tipped down the sink. The combination of time crystals and fizzy drink caused a rift in the time–space continuum, and, long story short, Meta and Merida spent the next three hundred and sixty-five days as French peasants during the French Revolution, in the late seventeen-hundreds. On the three hundred and sixty-fifth day, they were convicted of being sorcerers because of their digital watches and were being led up to the guillotine for execution. If you don't know what a guillotine is, then I'm afraid I can't tell you in a children's book. You'll have to ask your parents, but don't tell them why you are asking, or where you heard about it, because

I don't want to get angry letters about it.

So, as Meta and Merida were being led up to the guillotine, Merida said, 'I told you so.'

Luckily for Meta and Merida, just as the blade of the guillotine dropped towards Meta's neck, the lemonade in their kitchen sink *finally* went flat and they were instantly transported back to Huggabie Falls in the current time. The only injury Meta sustained was that one of the hairs on the back of his neck was sliced perfectly in half. But even so, while they were walking up to the guillotine, Merida had said, 'Meta, putting those time crystals down the sink was definitely not a good idea. I told you so.' And that was officially the absolute best moment to say 'I told you so' in the history of the universe. What's more, the time crystals were still moving down the drain, and were about to collide with an un-popped party popper next, which was going to send Meta and Merida forty-four thousand, nine hundred and eighteen years into the future.

Actually, when Felonious Dark Two said, 'There's never been a better time to say I told you so'—as the residents of Huggabie Falls were marching down the street arm-in-arm with their greatest fears—it was actually only the one thousand, four hundred and fifty-seventh best time to say 'I told you so'. But it didn't really matter, because the top-hatted scientist hadn't stuck around to hear it. He had dashed back into the House of Spooks and into the secret lab, leaving Felonious Dark Two to face the people of Huggabie Falls and their greatest fears alone.

Felonious Dark Two fixed his eyes on his brother, who was walking beside a rather threadbare teddy bear, a teddy bear that was cracking its knuckles. This confused Felonious Dark Two, as he didn't know teddy bears had knuckles, but he wasn't about to spend any time wondering about teddy-bear anatomy just then; he was more concerned that his three-fewer-letters-in-his-name brother was about to challenge him.

A large group of lab-coated scientists came running out of the House of Spooks. They obviously worked for the top-hatted scientist, who must have sent them out to fight off the people of Huggabie Falls and their greatest fears.

Felonious Dark Two looked at the scientists running out of the House of Spooks and held up a flat hand in a stop motion. 'Let's get them,' he said. 'Just as soon as I finish my mocktail—it's *extremely* tasty.'

Cymphany watched all this as she led the crowd of Huggabie Falls residents and their greatest fears, with Tobias, Brussels Sprout, Felonious Dark, Mr Puddles and Bugsplatter right behind her. 'The top-hatted scientist just ran back into the House of Spooks,' Cymphany said. 'And Mr Dark Two and a large group of rather evil-looking scientists are running towards us.'

Brussels Sprout raised a leafy, annoyed eyebrow at her. 'Aye. We can see that, Miss Obvious. We're lookin' at exactly da same thing that ye are.'

Cymphany smiled apologetically. 'Sorry. That's a thing I do—provide commentary. Come on,' she said, urging Tobias and Brussels Sprout to jump onto Bugsplatter's back, as Bugsplatter spread her wings ready for takeoff. 'We'll fly into the House of Spooks, deal with the top-hatted scientist and then save Kipp and his family and Conrad Creeps. Mr Dark, you and everyone else can deal with your brother and the lab-coated scientists.'

Felonious Dark looked at Felonious Dark Two and the scientists running towards them. He gulped. 'I guess. But what if having three extra letters in his name really does make him better than me?'

'Don't be silly, Mr Dark,' Tobias said, climbing onto Bugsplatter's back. 'And besides, why don't you just call yourself Felonious Dark One. Then you'll both have the same number of letters in your names.'

Felonious Dark's eyes went wide. 'I could do that?' His chest puffed out with a sense of pride.

'Felonious Dark One. A sixteen-letter name. I never dared dream I'd have a sixteen-letter name.'

He gave Tobias a swift nod. 'Go! Save your friends. We'll take care of my brother and the lab-coated scientists. Finally, my brother and I face each other as equals.'

Brussels Sprout was last to board Bugsplatter. Bugsplatter flapped her wings and lifted them into the air—just as the crowd of Huggabie Falls residents and their greatest fears met the crowd of scientists led by Felonious Dark Two like two rampaging armies on a battlefield.

22

The Really Big, Huge Mega Battle

There have been many great battles in history: the battle of Waterloo in the Napoleonic Wars, the Battle of Troy during the Trojan War, and one of the all-time most epic battles—the battle between the fans of the television series *Space Patrol* and the fans of the television series *Patrollers of Space* at the Huggabie Falls Science-Fiction Film and Television Convention, over which series had the more 'captainy' space captain.

But the battle that raged in the streets of Huggabie Falls that day put all other battles in history to shame. As you might have already worked out, it took place between the Huggabie Falls residents and their greatest fears and the newly named Felonious Dark One on one side and an army of lab-coated scientists (who were menacing, yes, but slightly less menacing than the henchmen the creepy scientist had helping her in the first Huggabie Falls book) and Felonious Dark Two on the other side. This battle had a Tyrannosaurus Rex in it for starters. Everyone knows that a battle with a Tyrannosaurus Rex in it is at least ten times more awesome than one without a Tyrannosaurus Rex in it. Sadly, T-Rexs have been absent from many of recent history's battles, which is largely due to the fact that dinosaurs became extinct sixty-five million years ago.

Also doing their best to make the battle more awesome were: charging bathtubs with rubber duckies in them; a flying witch on her broomstick turning scientists into bowls of custard; clowns riding tiny bicycles and jousting at the lab-coated scientists with French loaves, knocking them into spiderwebs spun by two-metre-tall spiders; pigeons pooing on scientists with military-strike accuracy and blinding them, enabling Huggabie Falls residents to lock those lab-coated scientists in blue plastic portaloos; and, in the middle of it all, a man reciting really bad poetry, like:

War, War, all around me.
What a bore.
When someone hits a golf ball they scream 'fore'.
Why don't they scream three?
It confuses me.

Amid the chaos, Felonious Dark One and Felonious Dark Two stood on opposite sides of Digmont Drive, hands poised by their sides as if they were two gunslingers in the Wild West. They eyeballed each other fiercely and were not distracted as an octopus made of feathers galloped past. That was Coach Peltin Pilkon's fear, but now Coach Pilkon was piggybacking on the feathered octopus, and the two of them were racing around the street unleashing tickle-bombs on lab-coated scientists until the lab-coated scientists were giggling so much that other Huggabie Falls residents could tie them up.

Felonious Dark One and Felonious Dark Two did not notice this or any of the other bizarre battles happening around them, as they were totally focused on each other. The poet, too, was transfixed. He looked at each of them in turn:

Felonious Dark One versus Felonious Dark Two—
I hope neither one of them steps in pigeon poo.

At last Felonious Dark Two spoke. 'Shall we settle this in the same way we've always settled our disputes, brother?'

Felonious Dark One nodded with the

extreme confidence of a man who now had sixteen letters in his name. 'You're on.'

This earned a snigger from Felonious Dark Two. 'You have not beaten me in forty years.'

Felonious Dark One shrugged. 'Well, today seems as good a day as any to change that.'

Some of the Huggabie Falls residents and their greatest fears and some of the scientists had noticed something momentous was going on, and they began to gather round. The poet clapped his hands together.

Two brothers wage an epic war.
Last one out should shut the door.

Tobias's mum, who was nearby, and who had a scientist in a headlock, heard the bad poetry and laughed. 'It's terrible but, you know what, it's growing on me. I can't believe I was ever scared of bad poetry.'

Felonious Dark One and Felonious Dark Two walked towards each other until they were

chest to chest. Each one's eyes were locked on the other's.

'The loser,' Felonious Dark Two snarled, 'leaves Huggabie Falls forever, and takes his army with him.'

Felonious Dark One nodded. 'Agreed.'

They each took a single step away from each other.

'Now draw,' Felonious Dark Two bellowed.

The poet gasped. The Huggabie Falls residents gasped. A ghost fainted. And even the Tyrannosaurus Rex tried to put his hands over his shocked mouth, but as T-Rexs only have little arms he just looked like he was trying to give someone a high ten.

The air in the street went still. A tumbleweed tumbled past. Everyone knew they were about to witness something extraordinary.

Mr Treachery, who was stealing a transfixed lab-coated scientist's wallet, whispered to Mrs Treachery, who took the wallet from her husband and put it in another transfixed lab-coated scientist's pocket. 'When is it going to start?' he said.

And then it started.

Felonious Dark One and Felonious Dark Two each whipped one hand up. The hands clasped together. Each man's fingers curled around the other's, locking the two hands together into a ball—a ball with two thumbs poking out the top. The thumbs bowed at each other, and Felonious Dark Two sneered. 'Last chance to give up, little brother. You've never beaten me. A few extra letters won't save you now. This will be the grand championship of thumb wars. Unless you're so terrified you want to surrender already.'

'I will never surrender,' Felonious Dark One said, with impressive determination.

Felonious Dark Two raised his free hand and roared, 'Let the thumb-war championship begin.'

And it began. The thumbs dodged and weaved and taunted each other. Every now and then a thumb would leap forward and attempt to squeeze the other thumb flat, but the other thumb would dodge free just in time.

'What are they doing?' the feather octopus asked Mrs Turgan, who was standing with her broom and holding eleven bowls of custard.

'*Arrrgh!*' Mr Haurik cut in. Somehow he had moored his ship, got a tub of popcorn, and was stuffing his face with it. 'They're having a thumb war. To win a round, you have to pin your opponent's thumb down for a count of three. First to win three rounds is the champion. *Arrrgh!*'

Felonious Dark One and Felonious Dark Two adopted side-on fencing stances, with their free arms aloft behind them for balance. They moved round and round in a circle, their eyes locked in intense concentration.

'It's a thing of beauty,' said one of the lab-coated scientists, despite the fact he was lying on the ground with Ms Suddlehoney's sloth sitting on his chest.

The entire town—including all the greatest fears and all the lab-coated scientists, most of whom had been overpowered, watched the thumb-warring brothers.

The epic duel waged on. These men were obviously thumb-war hotshots. A couple of times one thumb would sucker punch the other in the knuckle, and someone would scream out, 'Keep it clean.'

Suddenly, Felonious Dark One's thumb lunged. Felonious Dark Two's thumb tried to dodge, but it wasn't quick enough and, in a flash of thumbs, it was pinned. Felonious Dark One

shouted, 'One, two, three,' and then he roared in triumph.

(These four stars above are a little trick I've been told authors use when they want to switch to a new place, within a chapter. I doubt it works, but I like stars.)

Inside the House of Spooks, Cymphany, Tobias, Bugsplatter and Brussels Sprout didn't go to the secret lab, where they expected the top-hatted scientist would be hiding. Instead, they went straight down to the cells.

It came in very handy that Bugsplatter had acid saliva, as she was able to burn the locks off the cell doors. 'It also comes in handy for burning extra holes in belts,' Bugsplatter said proudly.

Bugsplatter sizzled opened the cell doors for Kipp's parents and Kaedy and Conrad Creeps.

'Thanks kids,' the voice of Kipp's dad said. Then Bugsplatter sizzled open Kipp's door and everyone expected him to come running out. But he didn't.

Cymphany and Tobias found their friend sitting cross-legged on the dirt floor of the cell, staring at a tall ornate mirror. Kipp didn't say anything. He just kept staring at the mirror.

'Kipp,' Cymphany said, kneeling beside him. 'We have to find that top-hatted scientist. Who knows what he plans to do next?'

But Kipp didn't take his eyes off the mirror. Tobias looked at it and frowned. 'How come I can see myself in the mirror, and you, Cymphany, but not Kipp?'

Cymphany looked in the mirror and saw that Tobias was right. Even though Kipp was sitting on the ground between them, in the mirror it was like he was—

'In the mirror I'm invisible,' Kipp moaned. 'The mirror is showing me my greatest fear, my horrible future. I don't want to turn invisible.'

Kipp wiped his eyes with the back of his sleeve. 'It will be like I'm not here at all.'

'Oh, Kipp,' they heard Kipp's mum's voice say from behind them. 'It isn't so bad. I mean, your father and I have the most epic games of hide and seek.'

'It's true,' Kipp's dad said. 'They can last for months.'

Despite the fact Kipp still looked sad, his parent's joke made him smile—just a tiny bit—but he was still hunched over. Cymphany put her arm around him.

'We know you're going to turn invisible one day, Kipp,' Cymphany said. 'And that's scary. But even if we can't see you, to us you'll always be here, and'—she smiled—'we'll always be here for you.'

'Always,' Tobias added.

Kipp looked at his friends and brightened up. He stood up and turned away from the mirror. 'C'mon,' he said. 'We've got a top-hatted scientist to stop.'

Tobias grinned. 'I've always wanted to say this,' he said, and he held a fist in the air and shouted, 'To the secret lab!'

(What do you know? The stars work.)

Outside, the thumb war raged on. The whole town crowded around and cheered their favourite player, and—considering the number of Felonious Dark Two banners being waved about—it seemed most of the crowd was cheering for Felonious Dark Two.

And the crowd was probably cheering for Felonious Dark Two because he was now winning. Felonious Dark One had started well and won the first round and then the second, but now the scores were even and in this the deciding round Felonious Dark Two was *obliterating* Felonious Dark One. A contest hadn't been this one-sided since a woolly mammoth once challenged a guinea pig to a pie-eating competition.

In anticipation of Felonious Dark Two's victory, someone had even managed to get *Felonious Dark Two: The Great Thumb War Champion* T-shirts made up, and most of the crowd was already wearing them.

Felonious Dark One and Felonious Dark Two still had their hands clenched together. Felonious Dark One was on the ground on his knees, and Felonious Dark Two was looming over him, gloating. He was especially good at gloating—he'd had lots of practice, having beaten his brother at everything they'd ever done in their entire lives.

Felonious Dark Two sneered at Felonious Dark One's bulging fearful eyes and the sweat running down his forehead. 'So,' Felonious Dark Two announced, 'I've won the last two rounds, with ease, and now I shall win the third and finish this contest once and for all.'

'You're cheating,' Felonious Dark One blubbered. 'It's like your thumb is twice as long as mine.'

'Our thumbs are exactly the same length, you nincompoop,' Felonious Dark Two snorted. 'We're identical triplets.'

Felonious Dark One had been ultra-confident when he'd won the first two rounds. But he wondered now whether his brother had only been letting him win to fill him with a false confidence so that his eventual loss would be even more humiliating.

After that, the next two rounds had barely lasted five seconds each. Now Felonious Dark Two was one round from victory, and Felonious Dark One's thumb was staggering with exhaustion.

'Let me remind you,' Felonious Dark Two

said, 'That whoever loses this round has to leave Huggabie Falls forever, with all your townsfolk and their greatest fears.'

And then, with lightning speed Felonious Dark Two's thumb launched and flattened Felonious Dark One's thumb, holding it down in an unbreakable grip.

Felonious Dark One tried to wrench his thumb free, but it was no good. He looked up into Felonious Dark Two's eyes, which were full of triumph.

Felonious Dark Two began the victory count: 'One.'

(I love these four-star breaks. I think I'll keep using them.)

Inside the House of Spooks, Tobias, Cymphany, Kipp, Bugsplatter, Brussels Sprout, Kaedy and Kipp's parents raced to the secret lab. Conrad

Creeps wasn't with them, because he had been too scared to leave his cell, plus he was also scared of racing, and secret labs, and final confrontations. Everyone agreed it really had to be tough being Conrad Creeps.

As they all burst through the door to the secret lab, they saw the top-hatted scientist. He was standing on a raised platform above the hard-light-hologram-generation machine. He wasn't wearing his top hat anymore—he was lowering the electronic flashing and bleeping cap, which was connected to the hard-light-hologram-generation machine, onto his bald head. The machine was humming, and the hum was getting louder and louder—it sounded like an aeroplane getting ready to take off. And the hard-light laser-shooting hairdryer things were glowing as if they were ready to burst into action.

'He's creating a scare-ball creature,' Kipp yelled.

'Correction,' the top-hatted scientist said,

although, as we've already established, he wasn't wearing his top hat right then. So maybe we should call him the electronic-capped scientist from now on. He spread his arms out wide. 'I'm creating the *ultimate* scare-ball creature.'

Tobias gulped. 'Okay, that sounds *really* bad. If he has just been creating non-ultimate scare-ball creatures up till now, then I'm not looking forward to seeing what an ultimate one looks like.'

The electronic-capped scientist sneered. 'You kids think you're so smart, convincing the Huggabie Falls residents to befriend their greatest fears. But wait till you see the unbelievably scary creature my imagination can create. Once everyone sees this creature, they'll run screaming from town and not even a raised drawbridge will stop them.'

The electronic-capped scientist closed his eyes and put his fingers to the sides of his head. He looked like he was straining and imagining hard. The machine was so deafeningly loud now, and the hard-light laser-shooting hairdryer things were beginning to form a meshed shape that was almost as high as the ceiling. As the shape took shape, everyone gasped.

'That looks flipping scary,' Brussels Sprout said in a very bad Scottish accent.

Even Bugsplatter's face went white with fear, and, considering her face was orange and purple before, that was a significant colour change.

Kipp gasped. 'I'm afraid he's right. One look at that and the residents of Huggabie Falls will run for their lives.'

Cymphany's eyes were darting desperately around the room. She rummaged in her satchel for something to help them—maybe a ladder or something they could use to get up to the top-hatted scientist. But hoping to find a three-metre ladder in a small satchel was probably a tad ambitious. The only thing she found was a sew-on badge from the Dinosaur Fearers Anonymous group. She had been given it by Truman Trotter, one of the DFA members who had been swallowed by the T-Rex and who had joined some other swallowed DFA members and formulated an unlikely but ultimately successful escape plan.

I'll have to take a moment here to write *Yippee*, because it's great news that Truman Trotter survived. Remember, he was the minor character in this story I was going to make a major character in a future story? So, that's brilliant news for my future writing aspirations, but I appreciate it's probably who-cares-can-we-just-get-on-with-the-story-now? news for you, so I'll get back to the story.

Truman Trotter had given Cymphany the badge when she had seen him trudging out of town still soaked in T-Rex stomach fluids. Truman had announced he was leaving the DFA and was going to join a quilt-making club instead, because quilts, generally-speaking, didn't eat people.

Cymphany frowned at the badge. 'Well, this is useless against that,' she said, tossing the badge aside. 'The top-hatted scientist is right. I can't imagine anything scarier than that monster.'

Bugsplatter must have agreed, because she fainted.

But Tobias was frozen—staring at the DFA badge Cymphany had just thrown on the ground. A curious expression was spreading across his face. 'I'll be back in a minute,' he said, and he raced out of the secret lab and down the hall.

Cymphany and Kipp looked at each other, and had another one of those millisecond, shared-in-a-glance conversations. I won't write out the whole conversation here, as it would take up at least four pages, but I'll just give you the abridged version, which was:

Where could Tobias possibly be going at a time like this?

If he's going to get more free popcorn, then he is in big trouble.

Outside, Felonious Dark Two roared, 'Two.' He had taken an extraordinarily long time between counting one and counting two in his final victory count. This was due to the fact he had Felonious Dark One's thumb clenched in an unbreakable grip, which ensured his victory. So he was taking his time and revelling in the moment immensely. Because he knew that once he counted the third count, his brother would lose, and he and all the residents of Huggabie Falls along with their greatest fears would leave town forever.

Felonious Dark One had initially struggled and strained trying to wriggle his thumb free from under Felonious Dark Two's thumb, but now he had given up and he hung his head and waited for the inevitable final count.

Felonious Dark Two cleared his throat. 'Well there is only one thing left to do,' he said. 'One more word for me to say. It contains five letters.'

Felonious Dark One counted in his head. Oh, drat, he thought. *Surrender* has nine letters.

Felonious Dark Two opened his mouth and prepared to say the five-letter word that would end it all. And there was nothing Felonious Dark One could do about it.

★★★★

Back in the House of Spooks the hard-light laser-shooting hairdryer things were finishing the final part of the unbelievably scary, unbelievably big creature the electronic-capped scientist was imagining.

Kipp, Cymphany, Brussels Sprout, Kaedy and Kipp's parents were huddled together and watching in complete terror. Bugsplatter, who had recently fainted, was just lying there. Tobias still hadn't come back, and if he was getting more free popcorn, then Kipp and Cymphany hoped he was bringing back enough for everyone.

The hard-light-hologram-generation machine's lasers had almost completed the unbelievably scary creature, when a voice from the side of the room said, 'Excuse me.'

They all looked at the owner of the voice. Even the electronic-capped scientist opened his eyes and looked.

It was Tobias, and he was standing with

Gertrude, Felonious Dark One's receptionist.

'What do you want?' the electronic-capped scientist snapped. 'I'm about to finish making this unbelievably scary creature, and I'd appreciate a bit of shush.'

'Gertrude wants to show you something she's been practising,' Tobias said. 'Don't you Gertrude?'

Gertrude nodded.

The electronic-capped scientist looked thoroughly annoyed. 'Can't it wait?'

Gertrude shrugged. 'It won't take a moment. I just wanted to show you this.' She sucked in the biggest, deepest breath, and she began to contort her face with trembling effort. Her lips flattened and stretched out sideways, forming a line. Then she clenched her fists while she lifted the edges of her mouth with her neck muscles, driving the thin line of her mouth into a U-shape. Sweat streamed down her face as she prised her lips apart to expose two rows of clenched teeth.

She was smiling. And she looked quite proud

of her smile, even as her head shivered and shook and her whole body started to spasm with the effort of holding her facial muscles in place.

The electronic-capped scientist's eyes widened with shock and he began to shake with fear. 'That,' he said, 'is the most terrifying thing I've ever seen.'

And as he stared at Gertrude, he didn't notice that the electronic cap had started beeping and flashing wildly and the unbelievably scary creature the hard-light-hologram-generation machine's lasers had been creating had evaporated. Now the machine's laser-shooting hairdryer things were buzzing into action, as if forming something new. And that something was what the electronic-capped scientist was now seeing, which was the terrifying sight of Gertrude smiling.

The lasers whirred all over the place, but they weren't forming anything. They started to jolt and fizz and spark, and smoke began to stream from the terminals around the platform.

The hard-light-hologram-generation machine's humming was super loud now. If it had sounded like a jet plane taking off before, it sounded like a fleet of jet planes taking off now, with a fleet of space shuttles warming up behind them.

Then one of the computer terminals exploded. The hairdryer things sizzled. And the machine roared even louder.

The electronic-capped scientist spun around. 'No!' he screamed. He had just realised what was happening. 'It must not create a hard-light hologram of that hideous smiling woman!' He climbed down from the platform and ran to the machine. 'She's way too terrifying.'

Gertrude's smile turned into a frown. 'Excuse me!' she said, looking very offended.

Cymphany and Kipp ran over to Tobias, and Cymphany wrapped him in a hug. 'Brilliant work, Tobias. You're amazing.'

Tobias blushed. 'It was nothing. I just figured that if the top-hatted scientist saw something even scarier than anything he could possibly imagine he'd be too scared to continue with his evil plan. And I immediately thought of Gertrude. No offence, Gertrude.'

Gertrude twitched with surprise. 'Hang on. My smile is *scary*? I thought it was quite fetching.'

Cymphany grinned. 'It's great, Gertrude.'

Gertrude looked relieved. 'Would you like to see it again?'

'No, thanks all the same,' Kipp, Tobias and Cymphany said in perfect unison.

Cymphany turned back to Tobias and grinned. 'I thought I was the only one who came up with brilliant plans.'

'Well, now it's my turn,' Kipp said. 'And my plan is we'd better get out of here, because I think the hard-light-hologram-generation machine is about to explode.'

Cymphany looked alarmed. 'Let's go. Run.'

'Eh, yes, run,' Brussels Sprout said, shaking Bugsplatter awake.

'Mum? Dad? Kaedy?' Are you guys still

here?' Kipp asked as he heard them running down the hall. Kaedy looked like she was flying, but she was actually being piggybacked by—judging by the height—Kipp's dad. 'We'll get Conrad and get out of here,' Kipp's mum's voice shouted back.

The electronic-capped scientist was scrambling around the hard-light-hologram-generation machine, tapping madly at the consoles, but it wasn't doing much good as the consoles were on fire. 'Not my machine,' he screamed. 'Not my beautiful machine. Please, don't blow up,' he cried as he gripped the electronic cap and squeezed his eyes tight. 'I'm thinking of a little puppy now,' he said, although no one could hear him, because the machine was so loud you couldn't hear anything except the noise of a machine about to explode, which sort of sounds like: *Wwooooooollllllllllllllllnnnmmmm-mmmmmmbeeoooooooooooooooooooooooo.*

Kipp, Tobias and Cymphany pulled the cap off the electronic-capped scientist's head—making him now the bald scientist—and dragged him away from the machine.

'My machine,' the bald scientist cried, oblivious to the fact his machine was making I'm-about-to-blow-up noises. 'If the machine is destroyed, all the scare balls will shut down and everyone's greatest fears will evaporate.'

Cymphany looked fearfully at Bugsplatter. And initially Bugsplatter looked shocked too, but then her nineteen eyes met Cymphany's two, and she nodded. 'Well, you always knew I was just a hard-light hologram.'

Brussels Sprout nodded too, and chuckled. 'Aye, Sprouts were nae meant ta last forever.'

'It's okay,' the bald scientist said, although it was still impossible to hear him because the machine was even louder now. 'That thinking-of-a-puppy-thing I was doing before, I think it worked. I don't think the machine is going to explode now.'

And then the machine exploded.

282

★★★★

Outside, Felonious Dark Two had managed to say, 'Thre—' which meant that he was one *e* away from winning the thumb war, when the hard-light-hologram-generation machine exploded, and the whole House of Spooks erupted in a giant explosion of wood and train tracks and smashed bits of hidden video cameras and shredded parts of warning signs, which scattered everywhere, and a wave of force knocked everyone off their feet.

Lying in front of the house, with bits of debris raining down all around them, were Cymphany, Kipp, Tobias, Kaedy, Conrad Creeps, the bald scientist, Bugsplatter, Gertrude and Brussels Sprout.

Kipp's parents were there too, but you couldn't see them—they were just two parent-shaped indentations on the grass.

They all got to their feet and ran clear of the still-crumbling remnants of the House of Spooks.

'I can't believe it,' Cymphany said to Kipp and Tobias as they all looked back at what was left of the house, which wasn't much. 'Did we just foil the bald scientist's plans?'

Tobias nodded. 'I think we did.'

Kipp chuckled. 'Well that was easier than I expected.'

But right then, as the once top-hatted, then electronic-capped, and now bald scientist had predicted, the lights on top of the scare balls began to flicker, and the greatest fears of the people of Huggabie Falls began to fade. Within moments you could see straight through Bugsplatter.

'No,' Cymphany yelped. She tried to wrap her arms around her greatest fear, as if she could protect Bugsplatter from vanishing, but she passed straight through her.

Bugsplatter smiled, exposing her razor sharp teeth, which didn't seem at all scary anymore. 'Cheerio,' she said. 'Thank you, Cymphany, for being my first ever friend. See you in your nightmares.' And then Bugsplatter evaporated in a small puff of hologram light. Right then, Cymphany became the first person in history to wish for her next nightmare to arrive as soon as possible.

And right beside where Bugsplatter had been a second ago, Brussels Sprout was almost gone too.

'Bye, Brussels Sprout,' Tobias said. 'I'm glad we sorted out that I don't want to eat you or any other Brussels sprouts.'

Brussels Sprout smiled. 'Aye, but we'll always have this.' And he threw a grand piano at Tobias. Tobias leapt out of its path, but the grand piano evaporated mid-flight, and when Tobias looked back, Brussels Sprout was gone too.

Down the street, everyone's greatest fears were disappearing, some giving their owners final hugs or shaking hands—if they were still solid enough to do so.

Mr Puddles was the last to disappear. He looked at Felonious Dark One, who still had his thumb pinned by Felonious Dark Two.

Mr Puddles put his thumb up. 'Don't worry, Felonious,' he said. 'You'll find a way.'

And then he was gone.

The residents of Huggabie Falls were picking up the inactive scare balls and examining them. They were finding it hard to believe that they ever contained anything scary.

Kipp was the only one not looking at a scare ball. He didn't want anything reminding him that he was going to turn invisible one day.

He sighed. 'It's over.'

'No,' Felonious Dark Two corrected him. He still gripped Felonious Dark One's hand and had Felonious Dark One's thumb clamped down in an even more unbreakable grip than he had it clamped before. 'I've still got a thumb war to win.'

Cymphany turned, confused. 'But what does it matter now? We've won.'

Felonious Dark Two sniggered. 'I'm afraid not, Ms Chan. Because if I win this thumb war, my inferior brother here'—he motioned to Felonious Dark One with his non-thumb-clamping hand, in case there was any confusion as to who his inferior brother was—'promised that if he lost this thumb war the people of Huggabie Falls would leave forever.'

The bald scientist, who had been looking quite dejected up until this point—probably because his hard-light-hologram-generation machine had recently exploded—suddenly looked a lot happier. 'Well done, Felonious Dark Two, you sly devil,' he said.

Cymphany raised a furious eyebrow at Felonious Dark One. 'Mr Dark! Why would you make a promise like that? With all the Huggabie Falls residents and their greatest fears with us, we had your brother and the lab-coated scientists completely outnumbered. There was no way we were not going to win this battle. So why would you bet we would all leave Huggabie Falls over a thumb war?'

There was a long pause. All the residents, who were already upset at having lost their greatest fears, now looked even more upset at

Felonious Dark One. They were probably all thinking what I am thinking, which is: why would someone so obviously terrible at thumb wars make such a promise?

Felonious Dark One grimaced. 'Well, in hindsight, now that you mention it, it does seem a bit foolish.'

Felonious Dark Two laughed. 'Foolish is your middle name.'

Felonious Dark One recoiled. 'Hey! It's pronounced *Full-ish*.'

Felonious Dark Two shrugged. 'It doesn't matter how it's pronounced. You're still going to lose. Now, I've lost my spot with my counting, so I'll have to start again. One,' he roared.

Cymphany looked desperately at Kipp. 'Mr Dark is going to lose,' she said. 'This is terrible.'

'Two,' Felonious Dark Two bellowed.

'Oh, goodie,' the bald scientist said, and he clapped his hands in glee.

'We've got to do something,' Cymphany said to Kipp and Tobias.

'I don't know if we can,' Kipp said.

Tobias looked similarly flummoxed. 'I'm still getting over the fact that Mr Dark's full name is Felonious Foolish Dark One.'

'It's pronounced *Full-ish*,' Felonious Dark One called out. He was still trying to wrench his thumb free from his brother's grip. But it was no good because the main characteristic of an unbreakable grip is its unbreakable-ness.

Felonious Dark Two opened his mouth to say three, and everyone knew that in a second it would be over.

At this point in the story, I'd like to point out that it's moments like these that I wish I wasn't writing a sequel to *The Extremely Weird Thing that Happened in Huggabie Falls*. Because sequels are never as good as their originals, and this one certainly isn't going to be, because the bad guys are going to win, and it's all because of a silly thumb war and a foolish promise. It's the sort of deplorable nonsense that only ever happens in sequels, which is exactly why people should never write them.

It's obvious what's going to happen, and you don't want to waste time reading an obvious ending. All I can do is apologise. Just stop reading this book right now, take it back into the bookshop and ask if you can swap it for a book that has a 'Good Guys Win Ending Guaranteed' sticker on the front. That sounds much better.

...

...

...

To anyone who is still reading at this point. I can only assume you are a glutton for punishment, or you're being forced to read this book as part of a school assignment. If so, I pity you, and you should pity me too, because I'm the one who has to write this tragic inevitable ending and endure the terrible reviews, like: 'Why did he have to give the main villain character an unbreakable grip so that the good hero character had no chance of winning the day? This author really painted himself into a corner. What a klutz.'

Anyway, I suppose we'd better get on with it. The quicker I finish this, the quicker the pain will be over. Just like ripping off a bandaid, which I never do, by the way. It's too painful. But that means I have bandaids on my knees that have been there for more than twenty years.

Now, where was I. Oh, yes, the horrid ending.

Once again, Felonious Dark Two didn't say the final count, 'three', straightaway. He was a big fan of extended gloating, it seemed.

'You are so pathetic,' he said to Felonious Dark One, who had lowered his head in shame. 'You could never beat me. You never have, and you never will.' Felonious Dark Two laughed. 'I can't believe you've started calling yourself

Felonious Dark One. What were you thinking? What difference does a few puny letters make? They're just letters.'

And right then Felonious Dark One's left eye twitched, and he looked up. 'You're right,' he said.

Felonious Dark Two stopped laughing and looked at Felonious Dark One. 'What?' he said.

And then the weirdest thing happened. In his moment of absolute defeat, Felonious Dark One lifted his head high, and he said, 'You're absolutely right.'

Felonious Dark Two was confused.

So were Cymphany, Kipp and Tobias.

'I'm confused,' Cymphany said.

'Me too,' said Kipp.

'Felonious Foolish Dark One,' Tobias said. 'Is no one else flabbergasted at how funny that is?'

But Felonious Dark One didn't look foolish right then. He looked confident.

'You're totally right, brother,' he said,

standing up straight. 'A few extra letters in a name doesn't make me better than you. Nor does it make you better than me.'

Then there was a crunching noise. It took everyone a moment to work out what it was. It was Felonious Dark One gripping Felonious Dark Two's fingers so tight that Felonious Dark Two's bones started to crack. Felonious Dark Two yelped in pain, and his thumb flew up as he tried to wriggle his hand out of Felonious Dark One's crushing grip.

But no sooner had Felonious Dark Two lifted his thumb than Felonious Dark One's thumb launched forward and flattened Felonious Dark Two's thumb in an unbreakable grip. Felonious Dark Two stared at the situation, as though he couldn't believe it was happening.

But Felonious Dark One could believe it, and he didn't waste any time gloating. He calmly counted, 'One. Two. Three.'

Cymphany, Kipp and Tobias stared in absolute amazement, and so did the residents of Huggabie Falls. They started clapping and cheering, because Felonious Dark One had won, which meant they could all stay in Huggabie Falls.

The bald scientist looked horrified. 'I can't believe it,' he said. 'We lost. We *lost!* This couldn't get any worse.'

Remember what I said at the beginning of this story about tempting fate? Well, the bald scientist was about to learn that lesson, *again*, because no sooner had he said, 'this couldn't possibly get any worse', than a piece of a warning sign—which had been launched into the air when the House of Spooks exploded, and had obviously been launched very high, because it had taken quite some time to come down again—came down. Right on top of the bald scientist's head, knocking him out.

23

The End of the Sequel Curse

To anyone who followed my advice in the last chapter and stopped reading this book, I would like to humbly apologise, because that chapter didn't turn out anywhere near as bad as I predicted it would. I'm fact it turned out pretty flipping fantastic.

Of course anyone who followed my advice in the last chapter wouldn't be reading this chapter now, and therefore wouldn't be reading my apology. They would be up to about chapter three in a book with a 'Good Guys Win Ending Guaranteed' sticker on the front, so they are probably having a wow of a time but, still, it's a shame that they missed out, and I feel partially responsible. In fact, I feel totally responsible. But you're still here, so well done you for not following my advice. The advice adults give is not always correct, in fact, it is only correct approximately sixty-two per cent of the time.

Kipp, Tobias and Cymphany had won the day, along with some help from their greatest fears, which they were no longer so terrified of, not to mention Felonious Dark One and his receptionist, Gertrude.

The residents of Huggabie Falls took their now-inactive scare balls home and put them on their mantelpieces, or in their safes or on their bedside tables, and hoped that one day they might find a way to reactivate them.

And the next day the mayor of Huggabie Falls presented Kipp, Tobias, Cymphany, Felonious

Dark One and Gertrude with keys to the city.

Now, usually when keys to the city are presented, they are just ceremonial items, but in Huggabie Falls' case, these were actual keys to the city. They unlocked every single door, gate, padlock and secret diary in the whole of Huggabie Falls—so they were very handy bits of moulded metal indeed.

At the key presentation ceremony, there was much photo-snapping and much shaking of hands, and Gertrude did a bit more smiling—which made some of the Huggabie Falls residents think about leaving town again. Kipp, Tobias and Cymphany's parents kept saying how proud they were of their sons or, in Cymphany's case, daughter or, as her father called her, My Little Princess, despite the fact that there was no royal ancestry in the Chan family tree, at least none that Cymphany had been able to find.

As Kipp, Tobias and Cymphany posed for photos for the *Huggabie Falls Gazette*, the mayor said, 'Congratulations, children. Along

Huggabie Falls GAZETTE

$3

SCHOOLCHILDREN HEROES SAVE TOWN AGAIN!

with Mr Dark and Gertrude, you have saved Huggabie Falls, *again*. And I think this time was perhaps even more spectacular than the first time.'

Kipp, Tobias and Cymphany looked at each other. 'You know what?' Kipp said through the clenched, unnatural smile he was putting on for the gazette's photographer, which was a smile almost as unnatural-looking as Gertrude's. 'I think he's right. This really was an amazing adventure. Perhaps even better than our first one.'

And as Kipp said this, I, as storyteller, was forced to sit back...

....

Sorry. While I was sitting back I was unable to reach the keyboard for a second there—I could only reach the full stop key, which is why I have all those full stops above.

I was sitting back for a moment to think about how Kipp was right.

It seems I was wrong about the bad guys winning in the last chapter, and I was wrong when I said readers should go and swap this book for another one, and now it seems I may also have been wrong that a sequel is never as good as the original.

But I'll let you be the judge of that. Or, perhaps I'll go and get the book assessed by a professional sequel assessor.

After the presentation by the mayor, Kipp, Tobias and Cymphany stood at the edge of the Huggabie Falls town square, where all the Huggabie Falls residents were celebrating. Even Conrad Creeps, who was no longer quite so scared of celebrations, was there. Cymphany rubbed her jaw. 'My face hurts from smiling so much in all those photos,' she said.

Kipp nodded. 'I feel like my jaw is made out of concrete now,' he said.

Tobias laughed. 'I haven't smiled this much since I found out Mr Dark's full name was Felonious Foolish Dark One.'

'*Full-ish*,' Felonious Dark One corrected him as he walked up. But he didn't look annoyed. He looked very happy. 'Well done, kids,' he said, and he shook their hands.

'And well done to you, too, winning that thumb war, Mr Dark,' Cymphany said. 'Sorry, I mean, Mr Dark One.'

Felonious Dark held up his hand. 'Please. Just call me Felonious Dark. No need to put the One on the end. Like my brother said'—he winked—'a few extra letters doesn't make any difference.'

Kipp nodded. 'I guess your other brother, Al, doesn't have to worry about his name now.'

Felonious Dark snorted. 'Woah. Woah. I said a *few* extra letters doesn't make any difference. I still wouldn't want to be Al. I mean, just two letters. That poor sap.'

Kipp, Tobias and Cymphany giggled. They

were just happy things were back to normal or, in Huggabie Falls's case, back to weird.

The Huggabie Falls police officer, Officer Snaildraw, was loading Felonious Dark Two, the bald scientist, who could now be called the handcuffed bald scientist, and all the other lab-coated scientists into a bus that had 'Express to Huggabie Falls Prison' painted on the side.

Kipp, Tobias, Cymphany and Felonious Dark watched in silence as the bus drove away.

Then Tobias looked thoughtfully at Felonious Dark and said, 'Mr Dark, first you threatened this town, with the help of a creepy scientist—'

'But now I'm reformed,' interrupted Felonious Dark.

'Yes,' Tobias continued. 'Which is great. But then your brother threatened this town, with the help of a top-hatted, then electronic-capped, then bald, and now handcuffed bald scientist.'

Felonious Dark looked back at him. 'Yes. What's your point?'

'Well.' Tobias bit his lip. 'Your family seems

to have a bit of a love/hate relationship with this town. I just hope that your other brother, Al, isn't going to come to Huggabie Falls and cause trouble next.'

Kipp and Cymphany looked at each other, and you could tell they both shared Tobias's concern. I shared their concern too, because while this sequel has amazingly broken all the rules of sequel quality and might even be better than the original—a fact which is soon to be confirmed by a qualified sequel assessor—third books in a series are, without exception, always complete garbage. And I wouldn't write one even for two truckloads of money. Maybe... three. No, what I am saying, not even three. I have standards, you know.

But Felonious Dark didn't seem worried. 'C'mon kids.' He chuckled. 'Let's go back to the party and celebrate.' And as they followed him back, he added, 'You don't have to worry about Al. I'm sure he'll never come to Huggabie Falls. And even if he did, he couldn't possibly cause any trouble. I mean, how much trouble can a guy with a two-letter name cause?'

And if I was worried before, then I am even more worried now, and so should you be. As, by saying that, Felonious Dark showed that he had obviously not learnt the lesson that has been repeated again and again throughout this book—a lesson that I hope you readers have now learnt—which is that it is never a good idea to tempt fate.

The end.

Book 3

Kipp, Tobias and Cymphany came to a small stone cottage with an overgrown garden around it. The cottage was dilapidated, as if no one had lived in it for years, but down a cobblestone path at the back of the garden was a small office surrounded by glorious rosebushes and geraniums. It was the opposite of dilapidated—I guess it was 'lapidated'.

Kipp, Tobias and Cymphany stood hesitantly at the door.

'I've heard he hasn't come out in years,' Cymphany said.

Kipp shook his head. 'He must have. How does he eat?'

Tobias looked worried. 'I've definitely heard he doesn't like visitors. I mean, look at that mat.'

Find out what happens next in Huggabie Falls in *The Utterly Indescribable Thing that Happened in Huggabie Falls*, out in March 2019.

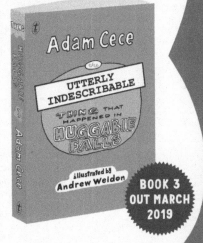